The Devil's Memories

By Vanessa Haney

Acknowledgements

Thank you, once again, to my early draft readers, to my son Connor, and to Mike. I truly appreciate the valuable time that you give so generously, and your encouragement means the world to me.

Author's Note

This is a book about vampires, witches, angels and demons and if you're with me so far, I assume you've already at least somewhat suspended your disbelief. That said, I did try to maintain historical accuracy when time traveling with you. However, I will confess here that I played with a few facts for creative purposes. For example, the deaths that occurred at Lake Pleasant were taken directly from local headlines but if there was a lake *monster* involved, that part of the story did not make the news.

Dedicated to all *women of a certain age*. May we maneuver through mid-life without having to drink the blood of our enemies (unless that's your thing).

Prologue

Arizona Territory 1864

It was hot. The sweat trickling down Adam's neck
soaked his collar and was absorbed by the already wet
patches of fabric clinging to his back. He would have
welcomed the breeze, except that it swirled the dust into
his eyes and ears and plastered a fine grainy film to every
inch of his exposed, damp skin. He took off his hat and
wiped his brow with a sleeve, smearing the grit across
his forehead.

The posse he'd been riding with had split up the day
before, and the men who stayed with him at the time
gave up that night. He turned in his saddle to see if
anyone had changed their mind, but he was still alone
in the desert. It was disappointing, but he couldn't judge
them for it. The Arizona summer could kill them just as
easily as a gunman could and the manner of death would
not be as mercifully quick as a bullet.

He might have given up himself, but there was
something different about the man they hunted. Walter
Sallow had tortured and killed two cowboys outside of

Tucson and then set fire to their camp. The lone survivor claimed Walter hadn't stolen anything or messed with the herd, he just seemed to enjoy hurting them. Adam was raised to be a god-fearing man and though he'd never seen any evidence of a god, he'd encountered plenty of evil. He knew that Walter's sort would spread through the area like a cancer if they let it.

Pulling the bandana away from his mouth, he said, "That's my good girl, Alice," and leaned forward to pat his horse's neck. She tossed her head in silent protest of their uncomfortable mission but after spotting a homestead in the distance, he nudged her forward. The heat coming up from the caked earth gave the small stucco house such a wavy appearance that Adam blinked a few times to make sure it wasn't just his imagination.

"Maybe those folks will be kind enough to give us some water."

Being much more agreeable than her namesake, Alice made a soft whinny and trotted off that direction.

A human shopkeeper, also known as Alice, was a mean thing who'd swindled Adam out of five dollars and he had meant it as an insult when he named his new chestnut Appaloosa after her. He'd gotten a good deal on the horse because the previous owner believed that her speckled white haunches were the cause of what he deemed an unseemly attitude in a four-legged creature.

Adam had braced himself for yet another troublesome female relationship, but the horse turned out to be sweet tempered and more loyal than most of his friends.

An uneasy feeling settled over him as they neared the house. A few chickens pecked around out front, there were horses in the stable, and he could smell a Mesquite fire out back. The name Carson was burned onto a wooden shingle that hung on the fence, and though nothing seemed out of order, everything about the place felt wrong.

Adam dismounted, hitched Alice to the fence, and drew his pistol. "Anybody home?" He called out.

"What do you want here?" The reply came with the double click of a lever action rifle as it cocked. From the side of the house stumbled a tall, skinny, brown-haired kid holding the rifle tight to his armpit and holding his other–visibly broken–arm across his chest. His eyes were wet and his whole body trembled from shock.

"Take it easy, son," Adam raised both hands over his head, making sure the kid saw that his finger was not on the trigger, "I won't hurt you."

"I'm not your son."

"Fair enough. Who do you belong to?"

"My name is Jess Carson, and I don't belong to anyone."

"Adam Colter," Adam said, lowering his hands. He glanced at the boy's arm. "What happened here?"

Jess stole a look in the window and a tear escaped down his cheek. He let the rifle tip forward and angrily wiped it away with his good hand. Adam could tell that the boy didn't trust his voice enough to speak, so he continued, hoping he was on the right track.

"I'm looking for someone," he said, gesturing at the broken arm, "someone I think you might have had the misfortune to meet."

"My grandpa." Jess squeezed his eyes closed. "He's in the house."

The sun shone through the large front window

across a table covered with a red and white checkered cloth. Neatly folded blue and green quilts draped the ends of two narrow beds lining opposite walls, and there were well used cushions made from the same checked fabric on the seats of two chairs that once sat on either side of the mantel.

The chairs were overturned and the small stacks of books that had been piled next to them were scattered across the floor. Even with the evidence of a struggle, it might have been a cheery place were it not for the headless corpse bleeding into the braided rug in front of the hearth.

Just inside the doorway Adam turned in a slow circle until he located the elder Mr. Carson's head, very nearly kicking it with his boot. Bile rose in the back of his throat and he stepped outside to catch his breath.

"I know how to fight." Jess looked down at his mangled arm as if still in disbelief. "But Mister ,that man is real strong and he surprised us in the middle of the night."

"Did he tell you his name?"

Jess shook his head. "He had these...these red eyes, though."

"Red eyes?" Adam arched an eyebrow.

"I ain't lyin'."

The surviving cowboy had said that Walter's eyes were 'red like a demon's'. Adam was no detective lawman, but he couldn't imagine that there were too many men fitting that description, so he knew he was close to running him down.

The sun was setting by the time they buried the old man.

Adam tried to give Jess some space at the gravesite behind the house, but the boy couldn't bear it so he found a thick branch and said, "We'll have to find a doctor to look at you—and soon, but this will do for now."

Other than a few pained grunts, Jess was quiet while Adam splinted his arm. Afterward, he announced, "I know you're going after that killer and I'm going with you."

"I thought you might say that, but—"

"But what?" Jess squared his shoulders. "I'm a man, just like you."

Adam looked him up and down. He had his doubts–the kid could not have been more than fifteen–but he asked, "Are you any good with that rifle?"

"Who do you think does all the hunting around here? My seventy-year-old Grandpa?" Jess clenched his jaw as he spoke of the dead man.

Adam clenched his jaw. He couldn't imagine what happened to the parents, but he could picture the boy and his grandfather reading those adventure stories by the firelight each night after the chores were done. Mr. Carson might have even been the one who taught Jess to read–a rare skill in the area.

"No matter what happens, this won't turn out like you expect it to," Adam warned. But Jess was already saddling his horse. He made it look easy, even with the use of only one arm.

They didn't talk much as they rode into town, but Jess couldn't help himself from asking, "You ever kill anyone?"

"Nope," Adam said, adding, "but I got a feeling Walter Sallow won't come along to be hanged without a fuss. Could be that changes soon."

"What if he kills you?"

Adam's lips thinned, but the kid asked a fair question. He'd been so furious since finding the headless man on the floor that he hadn't considered the possibility of Walter being the one to walk away from their encounter.

There was no hotel in town, but Jess had told Adam of a guest house and they planned to stay there, resuming the hunt at first light. When they rode past the saloon though, Jess pulled on his reins and said, "That's his horse." He would never forget the symbol etched into the saddle. It was a wolf's head with a long dagger plunged through its ears.

Adams turned to Jess, saying, "If he kills me and you've got a shot, take it. If you don't have a shot, then you better hide. Sell everything of yours and mine and get as far away from here as you can; do you hear me?"

Before he lost his nerve, he left Jess with the horses and pushed through the doors to the saloon. The bartender held up a bottle of whiskey and Adam nodded, sidling up in front of him. There were no girls, and no music, and as he looked around, he noticed that he and the bartender were the only ones in the place, except for one man at a table in the middle of the room.

The man spit tobacco on the floor and said, "You're all that's left of the posse."

Jess and the cowboy were right. Walter Sallow's eyes were rimmed with crusty, peeling flesh, as if he'd been sunburned over and over in the same spot, and they were bloodshot red. He had a large pendant of some kind hanging from a leather cord around his neck. He was bigger than Adam but not a particularly oversized man. Still, his gruesome appearance and arrogant mannerisms gave him the air of a titan.

Adam's mouth went dry. He was a good hunter and a damn quick draw, but he wasn't lying when he told the kid he'd never killed anyone. Not allowing himself to dwell on that, he turned to Walter slowly and said, "You're still under arrest."

"Take it outside," the bartender ordered.

"You put turpentine in the whiskey," Walter accused, and in a flash drew his pistol and shot the man behind the bar.

Adam had never seen anyone draw so fast, but even as the whiskey bottle shattered and the man collapsed behind him, he never looked away from his target, and he'd shot Walter in the stomach with his Colt revolver before the bartender hit the floor.

Walter roared and lunged for him, and as they fell backward through the swinging doors, Adam eyed the pendant around his neck. It was a dried-out wolf's ear, petrified and edged with crusted blood.

Adam scrambled away as they hit the boardwalk and Jess tossed him a rifle as he got to his feet. No man could survive for long after taking a belly shot, but there was Walter, flailing his arms and firing wildly into the street. He was going to kill everyone *but* Adam at that rate, and Adam had a sick feeling that was his plan.

Jess hollered, "Hey!" and drew Walter's fire in their direction.

Adam shot the rifle, cocked the lever, and shot again, over and over until Walter finally stumbled forward, face first in the dirt. His body convulsed, and he flopped onto his back, a pool of blood seeping out from underneath him.

"Finish it," he gasped, "or I'll come for you."

Adam gave Jess a doubtful look, but then he thought of the cowboys and old Mr. Carson, and he drew his pistol again, aiming it at the dying man's forehead.

"Finish it the right way," Walter rasped.

Jess was confused. "The right way?"

"His mind is gone already."

Walter reached out and grabbed Adam's ankle. "The right way," he repeated.

Never losing his aim, he jerked his leg away, and then Adam Colter held his breath...and killed a man. Or so he thought.

Chapter One

Present Day

He might not have noticed the dark-headed blur making its way toward the base of Shock Butte, but Sebastian Scott's gaze had been focused in that direction for twenty minutes as he watched the sun set over the mountains. Though he'd lived in the desert for most of his life, it never ceased to amaze him how the wide bands of gold and pink streaking across the sky made it appear as if the few clouds were ablaze.

As the evening's light show disappeared on the horizon, Bash reached inside the back door and took his binoculars from a peg on the wall. He twisted the focus and the figure of Adam Colter climbing the trail that wound around the butte became clear. Adam could move much faster than Bash, but not so fast that he couldn't be seen at all.

"What are you up to, Colter?" he wondered aloud.

As was frequently the case, Bash found himself torn between a longing to better understand his nocturnal friend and an instinctive inclination to stay out of the business of vampires. That night, he decided on the latter, replaced the binoculars, and locked the door behind him.

Safely inside, the most powerful of his instincts gave him pause. As one of Chuparosa's deputy sheriffs, he had a responsibility that went beyond mere curiosity. Adam's activities fueled his anxiety, but Bash trusted his friend and though Shock Butte was an odd choice, he reminded himself that for Adam, an early evening hike was no different than an early morning hike for the rest of them.

Lost in thought, he stood in the center of the room until Laura Deane looked up from the kitchen table.

"You okay?" She was sorting dried herbs and funneling them into linen pouches. Despite their many recent distractions, her herbal tea business was thriving and she would be up all night preparing her latest order.

The Duran Duran playlist had ended so he scrolled through her music app, turned the phone to show her his selection and when she grinned, pressed play.

"What else can I do, baby?"

She handed him a scoop and as Depeche Mode filtered through the little hockey puck shaped speaker on the table, he sat across from her and got to work, pushing Adam's behavior not out of, but to the back of his mind.

* * *

"Almost two hundred years," Adam announced to the night. He pulled a fifth of whiskey from his backpack, took a sip and sat down cross-legged with his back against the stone marker. "And I still ran out of time."

The angel known as Daniel had been buried atop Shock Butte by Heaven's Watch a few weeks earlier and it was only since then that Adam could finally talk to him on a regular basis.

Daniel's race of angels was called the Authorities. They led teams of humans against ancient forces that were inclined to take back the earth which they believed was stolen from them by an unjust god.

Adam had moved to Chuparosa shortly before Daniel began recruiting his friends into Heaven's Watch. The Deane sisters and their kids, Deputy Sebastian Scott, Deputy Chuck Ruiz and his wife, Mena, and Pastor Andrew Clarke. Their unfortunate life experiences and uncanny abilities made them excellent candidates for such a dangerous job.

On the surface they were only foot soldiers for a paranoid god that they were never even likely to see. In truth, they cared less about His agenda than they did about protecting the earth and those they shared it with, whether their neighbors were human or not. The ancient town of Chuparosa was built along a network of ley lines that ran through Arizona, and it was home to several direct portals that led to what the locals called the Other Side.

Chuparosa was rough, just ask Sheriff Scott, but its people were strong—they had to be. Both Sides existed by maintaining an uneasy truce over the years and though their collective moral compasses often spun wildly, Adam had always found himself in sync with the residents, no matter what Side of the veil they occupied.

It took some time, but they had more or less welcomed him, fangs and all, and it wasn't long until they were as devoted to him as they were to each other.

Daniel had never officially asked for Adam's help in the Watch, but he'd never refused it either. Adam's real interest in the angel always had less to do with the Lord's work than his own existential questions. Questions that would haunt him for his entire life, however long that turned out to be. With Daniel gone, there were no answers to be found and sometimes Adam feared that fact would drive him insane.

As a vampire he could see spirits and had been spending time near the grave in hopes that Daniel's ghost might haunt the area where he was murdered. Perhaps it was true though when Thomas said that angels, having served their purpose, simply ceased to exist.

Adam chuckled to himself. Of course, they would be left with Thomas, a fallen angel who once used a troubled young witch to father the Deane sisters. Even though he'd redeemed himself somewhat, everything Thomas said was to be taken with a lot more than a mere grain of salt. Adam ran his hand over the gravestone with a heavy sigh. Daniel's fate seemed unconscionable, but then again so did everything else.

He scanned the area once more for a hint of Daniel's presence but saw nothing other than two curious bobcats poking their heads around a crumbling rock formation. The Bobs lived on the Other Side but frequently wandered in and out of Chuparosa's many portals. Adam wasn't sure when they'd befriended the Watch, but they'd been a steady presence, if not an altogether comforting one, for as long as he could remember.

He was suddenly reminded of their mistress, Adira, and sat up straight to look around for her. The enormous mountain lion was more worrisome, but she was nowhere to be found that night, so he leaned the back of his head against the gravestone and tried to relax. The Bob's sniffed around him for a bit and then settled themselves in the dirt at his side. He gave one a scratch under the chin and checked his phone. Nothing from Cara either.

Cara Marshall used to accompany him in the desert at night, but she had declined once again citing a lead to follow up on. Like him, she hunted only 'monsters' for blood and her favorites were sexual predators. He feared it was becoming an obsession of hers, one that could cause unnecessary exposure and put both of them and their friends in danger.

He sat for a while longer, engulfed in the sounds of the desert at night. Between the dulling effect of the whiskey and the constant chirp of the insects, he nearly dozed off. In the distance, a group of coyotes began to yip at one another, and a sudden uneasy feeling jolted him out of the haze. The Bobs scattered as he jumped to his feet, convinced of another presence with him on the butte. But even with his heightened senses he could see nothing.

"Daniel?" He called out.

When there was no response, he snickered to himself in embarrassment, sent a two-word text and then made his way down the side of the butte. Unless there was an emergency, his job as night engineer at the utility company didn't require him on weekends, so on the way home he busied himself by mentally making plans.

There was a time when he volunteered at the hospital on the east side of Phoenix. It gave him a chance to balance all the violence in his life, but they'd had a change in administration and were only accepting daytime help. It was just as well since lately the violence might very well follow him in to one of the wards. Bash had said something about night fishing Saturday on Lake Pleasant and maybe he could convince Cara to come back to the butte with him on Sunday.

There were few streetlamps in Chuparosa, but as he approached his home in the moonlight, Adam could make out the figure of a man emerging from behind the shed in his yard. The man was half hidden, little more than a shadow and for a second Adam thought it might just be part of a Palo Verde tree. Then the shadow spit on the ground and a chill ran up Adam's spine.

He stole a glance toward the driveway and was relieved that Cara's car was still gone, but when he looked back, so was the intruder. There was something familiar about the man's behavior that filled Adam with dread and he sprinted to the shed, finding only footprints and a sickening glob of wet tobacco in the dirt.

Chapter Two

Cara found Jason in the bookstore's coffee shop with his nose buried in the latest C.J. Box novel. Jason had been her assistant at the bank and continued to moonlight for her when she left to start her own financial consulting company.

"Please tell me you're not going to run off and become a game warden," she teased, "Jason, I will die without you."

"Here." He frowned and handed her a double espresso. "I could never."

In truth, he dreamed nightly of doing just that but couldn't stomach the idea of wasting his expensive finance degree. The fact that she was a vampire and needed him in order to operate during the daytime notwithstanding, mentors like Cara were hard to come by. At the very thought of leaving her—or vice versa—he would pop a Tums.

She trusted him completely and was teaching him everything she knew, which was a lot. So much that when she left the bank, many clients begged her to take them along. The few who knew she was a vampire didn't care as long as their wealth continued to grow. Those who didn't know probably wouldn't have cared either since they never even questioned her odd meeting hours.

Her intent that night was to work for a while and then follow up on a rumor she'd heard about an abandoned building being used to process girls for trafficking. After some internet research, it looked like there wasn't much to the rumor since the police had recently done a decent sweep of the area in question.

She was weighing her decision to investigate further when Adam's text came in: `miss you`.

Her heart sank. She hadn't done either of them any favors by neglecting him lately and was suddenly quite anxious to get home. After responding to a few emails, she made some changes to a spreadsheet, finished her espresso, and closed her laptop.

Jason looked over his glasses. "Are we done already?"

"It's Friday night. Go have some fun."

"Like what?" He scowled at the foreign concept.

"Like a movie or," she lowered her voice for dramatic effect, "a girl." She laughed out loud at the pained look on his face. "Speaking of, do you want my man to get jealous?"

Jason gulped. He'd met Adam several times and no, he did not want to make him jealous. There *was* a girl he could call. A girl he'd disappointed by working that night. If she were still interested, they might be able to catch a movie. When he hurried off, Cara gathered her things, purchased an iced mocha for Adam and headed out.

Unlike the Deanes, her dark-headed statuesque friends, Cara was petite and blonde but since becoming a vampire, she could easily fight off any human attacker. Still, out of habit she positioned her keys between her fingers and scanned the parking lot for signs of trouble. It was a busy location with lots of friend groups and couples filing in and out of the restaurants, the book shop and the theater.

There was, however, one woman who stood out in the crowd. She was also petite, with lavender colored hair bobbed at her shoulders. She wore dark blue jeans and a pink t-shirt that said *Feminist AF*. She stared at Cara for a long moment and then smiled, flashed her fangs, and climbed into a deep red Ford F-150 with the license plate: R3DN3K. She waved out the window as she drove away, and Cara fell against her little Honda Civic in shock.

She drove home slowly wondering whether or not she should tell Adam about the woman and made an abrupt decision in the driveway, deciding to wait. Worrying him would defeat the purpose of her early return home. There had been no harm done and clearly, she and the other vampire were on the same side of society. If the woman showed up again, Cara would approach her and get some more details. Until then, she would try to resuscitate her relationship and use a bit more caution while she was out.

Even after a thorough search of the property revealed nothing unusual, Adam's anxiety level rose. He stared out at the darkness from behind the living room curtain, silently cursing himself for not pursuing an unsettling experience he'd had a few weeks earlier.

On the night that Daniel was killed, Adam's friends did battle in a church filled with demons while he headed off a group of goblins encroaching from the Other Side. Adam harbored a particular hatred for goblins and smiled to himself, remembering the satisfaction of tearing out their sinewy throats with his fangs.

His smile faded as the complete memory came back. The fire from inside the church had reflected off the windows, causing him to squint and as he tossed one of the short, scaly bodies away, he could have sworn that he saw the face of his maker in the refracted light.

The sight of him had given Adam such a jolt that he was unaware as the last goblin, emboldened by his paralysis, ran up behind him. He heard a wet crunch and a warbling squeal and when he whirled around, the goblin had been torn apart by someone else. Like his experience at the shed near his house, no one was there when he searched the land around the church.

"Shit," Adam growled.

Every decade or so they ran into one another. It was a pattern that he'd long since tired of and it was a dangerous complication that neither Cara nor his friends deserved to be saddled with. He could keep it from them while he figured out what his maker wanted this time but if he couldn't take care of it, they would be forced to deal with Walter Sallow on their own while grieving Adam's death.

Carl, his one-eyed brindle Pit bull paced alongside of him in a show of never-ending support, even though he resented being left home to wait for Cara while Adam hiked the butte. Carl lost his eye during a dog fight in Phoenix and had been left for dead by his handlers on the night Adam found him. By the next morning Carl was safe in a new home and a once lucrative criminal enterprise had suffered a bloody and permanent shutdown.

Adam had to stop himself from running out to meet her when Cara's car pulled in the driveway. Once inside, she piled her things on the coffee table and wrapped her arms around him.

"I miss you too, Adam."

His surprise at the notion brought tears to her eyes, but his hungry kisses told her that it would soon be okay. He seemed so relieved to see her that she took advantage, purring, "Do you want to go outside?"

He hesitated, tilting his head side to side and seeming to take great pains over the decision. A lock of dark brown hair fell across his eyes giving him the look of a boy who was up to something. He was every inch a man though, a man who had something on his mind, something she hoped it wasn't too late to fix.

In the end, he decided to keep whatever it was to himself, grabbed a throw blanket off the couch and opened the door. Outside, he took a long and careful look around before taking her hand and setting off into the night.

The moon was high overhead by the time they'd hiked to their favorite spot. It was a collection of large flat rocks, piled randomly and jutting over the side of Ford Canyon. The vast darkness was punctuated only by the outline of cactus in the starlight and the rustling of tiny animals scurrying around the bushes. Precariously close to the edge, he stood in silence with his back to her, and she worried that he might be having second thoughts about forgiving her inattention.

He soaked in the still night air for a while longer and then said, "I almost find it hard to miss the daytime when there are nights like this," He added to himself that he would do anything to preserve those nights and the life he and Cara had carved out in Chuparosa.

Then he felt her arms around his middle and his thoughts became more carnal. She walked her fingers up his chest and worked her way back down, undoing the buttons on his shirt until she reached his waistband and unbuckled his belt.

He moved her body to face one of the larger rocks and from behind brushed her hair aside to kiss her neck while he slid one hand down her shorts, and the other one up her sweatshirt.

She stepped one foot on a dead Saguaro branch, spreading her knees slightly and grinding against him as he slipped his fingers inside of her. When Cara could take it no more, she wriggled out of his grasp and knelt to take him into her mouth.

He buried his hands in her hair, relishing her softness. When he feared he'd lose control he lifted her to standing, tugged off her shorts and pushed her gently against the rock. She pulled him between her legs, tilting her hips to meet him as she pressed her feet against a mesquite tree for leverage.

As he slid into her, she lowered her fangs and let one sink into his earlobe. He hissed from the pain and yanked on her hair. When her head fell back, he ran his tongue all the way down to her collarbone.

As they moved together, he slipped his hands over

her bottom pulling her harder and harder against him. His woodsy scent was intoxicating, and she wrapped her arms and legs around him, submitting completely as his thrusts intensified and their mounting pleasure overtook them.

Staring into her gray eyes, he held her legs tight around his waist as their bodies shuddered against one another. He needed to tell her so much, but he wanted to savor their time together. Rather than trying to find the right words, he laid her down on the blanket and cuddled her to his chest.

Cara looked up at the stars and wondered about the lavender haired vampire. Adam told her once that he'd met a few other vampires but most of them were content to ignore him and were anxious to get out of sun-baked Arizona. Could it be that the one who drove the red truck was a permanent resident? If so, their lives would soon be dramatically different, but she would have to worry about that later.

Adam had been so lost in thought himself that he jumped when she said his name. Her chest tightened a bit as something in her knew that things between them were changing and it went beyond his hurt feelings.

Just out of sight, the man who had followed them through the desert turned away with a sneer and spat tobacco in the dirt.

Chapter Three

"You asshole." Bash set his tackle box on the dock and put his hands on his hips. "I thought we were going fishing tonight," he griped, "and you said you had a boat."

"This *is* a boat," Sam Parker's booming voice called up from a vessel clearly commandeered from the Sheriff's Lake Patrol. "And we *are* going fishing," in a quieter voice, he added, "probably."

Adam and Bash climbed aboard with their good friend, Deputy Chuck Ruiz; all of them frowning as they stowed their gear.

"I was unaware that Lake Pleasant had anything larger than striped bass," Adam said, picking up a spear gun from the bench.

Chuck took it from him and shook it at Sam. "Fishing for what, man?"

"Good to see you guys again!" Their former co-worker, Deputy Seth Ryder, stood at the helm with his hand out. Bash gave it a rough shake and then turned on Sam.

"Mother fucker," he fumed, "what are you playin' at tonight?"

"Before you go off the rails," Sam argued, "there's someone who wants to meet you. Officially."

"Ho-ly shit," Bash whispered as Nick Scott nervously stepped out of the shadows.

The last time they'd seen each other Nick was wild eyed, hunched over and grotesque, with long stringy hair and fingers that twisted into sharp claws. He had been hexed by Jaya, an angry Nephilim who used him as a pawn to get to Heaven's Watch. Bash had only learned of his brother's existence a few weeks before that when their estranged father showed up out of nowhere begging him to help the young man.

Since then, they'd broken Jaya's spell, and Sam's resources had apparently done wonders for Nick. He'd gained some weight and looked healthy and strong. His hair was cut short, and he stood up tall, lifting his head to meet his big brother's eyes for the first time.

Bash took him by the shoulders and looked him up and down. "Are you alright?" He grabbed his wrists to inspect his hands, which were back to normal.

"I recognize you," Nick started, "and I know who you are." He furrowed his brows. "I just don't remember everything...only a few horrible scenes."

"That's a good thing, man," Chuck assured him.

"And Jaya—" Nick whispered her name, looking around as if she might re-appear.

"She's dead," Bash confirmed quickly.

"When we fought..." Nick's face twisted from the pain of the memory, "did I hurt you?"

The wounds across Bash's chest still burned, but he said, "No."

Though everyone else knew Bash was lying, a heaviness lifted from Nick's shoulders, and his relief was so evident that they didn't even give the older brother a questioning glance.

Bash nodded his thanks to Sam but would not forgive him for luring them into what was sure to be, at best, an unpleasant operation. Reserving judgment until he figured out what Sam was up to, he instead turned his own inner asshole loose on Seth.

"Have you been to Jerome lately?" he teased, gesturing at the scars down Seth's arms, "or did you break up after the last intimate encounter?"

"Shut up," Seth grumbled, "I didn't know she was a cougar."

Nick's eyes widened. "You had sex with a cougar?"

"I said, I didn't know she was a cougar."

"No," Nick reminded him, "you told me those scars were from a fight with a wild animal."

"Oh, she was wild alright," Bash snorted.

"Seth," Adam was pretty sure that, considering the present company, he knew the answer, but still felt compelled to ask, "by cougar, do you mean an older woman or the—"

"He means the cat!" Bash threw his head back laughing so hard that he almost fell over the side.

Sam's expression sobered and he held tight to Bash's arm. "Careful now."

"What? I've got my vest on."

"That doesn't seem to matter."

Chuck sighed, "Why don't you tell us why we're really out here, man."

"Alright, alright...three weeks ago," Sam began, "a man drowned after falling from a jet ski. The week after that, a young swimmer disappeared. Then last week, a woman was caught in the propeller blade after slipping from the stern of her boyfriend's fishing boat."

"And this Thursday," Seth added, "an old fisherman went missing from the shore."

"Drunks get hurt out here all the time," Chuck said.

"True," Sam acknowledged, "and there were no signs of foul play until the woman with the propeller injury. Before bleedin' out, she told the paramedics that something reached up and pulled her over the side."

At one time Chuck and Bash worked with Sam and Seth as part of a special division of the county sheriff's department that kept track of Arizona's supernatural elements. While unfortunate and unusual, Chuck couldn't see why those cases warranted that unit's involvement and he certainly couldn't see why Sam would call them from Chuparosa to help.

"How did you guys get sucked into this?"

"The victims seem to be random, but it's the timing of the attacks—once a week. Every Thursday," Sam explained, "and other than the woman chewed up in the propeller, they can't find the bodies."

Bash moved farther away from the side of the boat. "None of them?"

"Not one."

"Do you think they were kidnapped?" Adam asked.

"Well," Sam smirked, "when Seth's not sleeping with shapeshifters, he's reasonably good at research and he thinks the conditions are right for the Chersydros."

"Seriously?" Chuck was not convinced. "We haven't had a Chersydros in over twenty years."

"Hey, I'm just telling you how the stars are lining up." Seth opened an old book and shined a flashlight on the pages. "You don't hear of them very often because they're usually content to stay in the way deep, but the water levels out here have dropped quite a bit from the drought and there are fewer fish to keep it busy. More boats are on the lake than ever, which is great for tourism but—"

"Probably seen as an intrusion by the local monster population," Chuck finished.

"I'm not gonna lie, the budget is tight, and I could use the help," Sam admitted.

"You brought my brother into this?" Bash's annoyance was renewed, but Nick proudly pointed to his badge and pulled his shirt back to reveal the sidearm he carried.

"Are you fucking kidding me?"

"What else am I gonna do with my life?" Nick asked him.

"You could move to Chuparosa and have a normal—" Bash stopped himself, realizing how ridiculous it would sound if he completed that sentence.

"If we don't get killed," Sam offered, "I'll owe you one."

Chuck looked up from the book and said, "One?"

"Okay, one each."

The men went quiet while they reviewed the legend until an owl hooted from the trees on the shore, jolting them from their thoughts.

Seth closed the book and said, "I think it's grabbing the sides of the boats to tip people out and drowning them as it takes them away."

"Takes them where?" Adam asked.

"The low water levels have exposed some caves on the other side of Tartor Bay and we believe it's moved into one of those. Public access to that area is closed for conservation so it would make a pretty good hunting base."

Sam stared out at the darkness with his back to the others as the boat moved swiftly through Jackass Cove. He'd considered waiting for a better time to conduct his interrogation but decided to risk Sebastian's wrath and go for it.

"I don't know why Adam couldn't just pull that information out of Seth's mind."

Chapter Four

Jackass Cove was aptly named, not for the reckless jet skiers but for the many wild burros whose braying echoed across the lake. Even so, Bash would have named it for Sam that night.

"Aaaand there it is," he snapped, "I could have counted down to when you would start asking stupid questions."

Adam was the only one in the group who was unaffiliated with the sheriff's department, and Bash had a feeling from the start that he wasn't invited along that night just to make new friends.

"What?" Sam's tone was playful, but he clearly had an agenda. "I'm just curious. Fangs aren't necessarily the most interesting thing about a vampire."

"It's alright, Sebastian." Adam figured Sam had been dying to question him since they met the month before, but Bash was defensive of his friend.

"Dammit Sam."

"Just let the man talk. I'm not used to hearing directly from the creatures I, uh, encounter."

"Before you kill them, you mean?" Adam wondered.

"You're not already 'undead'?" Sam made air quotes with his fingers.

"I prefer the term 'undying'," Adam said, "but that's not really true either because I can be killed." He was determined not to squirm under the scrutiny, but it was going to be a difficult conversation for him.

"You're among friends here," Sam assured him.

"So it would seem." Adam eyed a second spear gun and various other implements on the boat that could be used as a stake but decided to offer trust as his first line of defense.

"First of all, I'm a human being, just like you. Someone used my humanity against me to give me this condition."

"Condition? Talk to me about your condition."

"I do need blood to survive but not every night–any vampire who tells you that is a liar. We can go weeks without it. I'm faster and stronger than you but I will burn up in the sunlight."

"Is that the only other way to kill you, besides a stake?"

"Is that not enough for you?"

"Let it go, Sam," Bash warned.

"Can you fly?" Nick asked.

"No."

Nick couldn't hide his disappointment, which made Adam suddenly wish that he could, but he compensated by offering, "I can see spirits...or ghosts, if that's what you want to call them."

"Before you ask," he looked at Chuck and Bash, "Cara cannot see them, but her other senses are even keener than mine. I was very sick when I was turned so that might have something to do with it."

"Sick?"

"Typhoid."

"Jesus."

"Everyone in my bunkhouse was afflicted, but that was no surprise given the conditions at the time."

Nick scowled. "You were attacked when you were sick?" He was particularly sensitive to such behavior since he'd been near death himself when Jaya's minions found him.

"Well, that's part of a much longer story son, but yes—I was dying."

"So, by making you a vampire, he saved your life?"

"I suppose whether or not I agree with that statement depends on the day, but I can assure you that man had no kindly intentions when he did it."

"Here we are." Seth made the announcement in little more than a whisper as he pulled around Tartor Bay.

"Ugh, god." Nick gagged from the stench carried on the breeze.

"Yeah," Bash said through gritted teeth, "I guess we've found the bodies."

Seth dimmed the lights, beached the boat, and folded down the bow door. They jumped off and found the old fisherman just inside the mouth of the cave. When Chuck knelt for a better look, Adam pulled him back up.

"Wait," he said.

His senses might not have been as keen as Cara's, but they were much better than the others' and, in the pitch black of the cave, Adam could see the outline of the creature, at least seven feet tall, wading in a pool of stagnant lake water against the back wall. It had the look of a salamander standing upright on stubby hind legs with a thick tail curled around it; the end draped over a clawed arm. Three tendrils of villi growing out from its gills shrouded four long fangs, two upper and two lower. It smacked those jaws when it saw them and its long, barbed tongue slipped out like a snake's, wriggling at the air.

"I can't see it." Sam aimed the spear gun, but he was too low, so Adam raised the barrel for him.

"Well, it can see you," he cautioned.

The others pulled their pistols and flanked Adam on each side. The creature let go of its tail, getting ready to strike.

"You got that spot lamp?" Chuck asked Seth.

The creature hissed as Seth flicked it on, then whipped its tail around, catching Seth behind the knees and smacking the back of his head against the rocky floor. The lamp flew from his hands, still shining but facing away from them on the other side of the cave.

"Get him out of here!" Sam shouted, and while Nick was dragging Seth's unconscious body away, the tail whipped around the other direction and knocked the spear gun from Sam grip. Then it flicked its tongue over and over so quickly that, in the dim light, Chuck never saw it coming before the jagged spikes punctured a bloody trail down his chest.

Adam tore the spear away from the gun and, with all of his speed and strength, rushed at the creature, pinning it to the wall. It gurgled and slashed its tail, throwing him backwards into Bash who, from the ground, shot it through the gills with the other spear gun. Sam rose to his knees and, from as close as he dared, emptied his pistol's magazine into the creature's slippery green torso.

It flicked its tail one last time and then slumped forward with its tongue sliding into a puddle of drool that oozed from its slack jaw.

"Jesus Christ," Bash grumbled. He ripped open Chuck's blood-soaked shirt to reveal at least half a dozen seeping stab wounds.

"I hope I'm not allergic to that thing." Chuck tried to laugh, but it came out as more of a wheeze.

After many phone calls and what Bash considered to be an unreasonable wait time, Chersydros or no, the paramedics finally arrived. They busied themselves with Chuck and Seth while he led the coroner through a maze of half-chewed bodies in the cave. The coroner's assistant seemed unbothered, flashing a toothy smile and turning his baseball cap backward before crouching over what was left of the missing swimmer.

Never one to waste time, Sam took the opportunity to ask Adam another question. "What do you know about the vigilante activity in the sex worker community downtown?"

Cara had made that area her hunting ground, but Adam shrugged and shook his head.

"That's fair, I guess." Sam knew he was lying and Adam knew that he knew, but silent communication was a game they would have to play to protect Cara. Sam had to admit that losing a few violent offenders off the street wasn't the worst thing, but he made sure with his expression that Adam understood it must be kept in hand. And since Adam had been forthcoming up to that point, Sam decided to return the favor.

"As a rule, I like to let sleeping vampires lie, but rumor has it that Pinetop has a new nest."

Adam inhaled sharply. Sam referred to an incident involving renegade vampires that he, Chuck and Bash once hunted up north.

"Yep." Sam made a face and wiped some Chersydros slime on his pants. "I'm told that there are scouts up there now, making ready for the master. These aren't nice guys like you," he couldn't keep the sarcasm out of his voice, "so keep your hyper-functional eyes and ears open."

Chapter Five

"Chersydros," Cara repeated Adam's word back to him over the phone. "We have those?"

"Apparently." His voice sounded distant, even for Lake Pleasant's sketchy cellular reception.

She wrestled with the urge to demand that he return to her instantly. They could take a trip down south and reconnect for a while, or maybe just set up some couples counseling. Surely they could pay David Trainer enough to meet with them at night. As far as she knew, he'd had no vampire experience, but as Chuparosa's only licensed therapist it was time David expanded his resume to meet the diverse needs of their community.

Instead, she settled on a few choice words of disdain for Samuel Parker, adding, "Laura should hex him for tricking you guys like that."

"Well, the thing is dead, but it'll take a while for Chuck and Bash to wrap things up here."

"Just be careful." Cara ended the call astonished by her hypocrisy, considering what was about to happen. Since he was going to be *fishing*, she'd privately made plans of her own.

As it turned out, she had needs that Adam simply could not meet and since he couldn't help her, she decided not to burden him with them. Like her, he only hunted the worst criminals against humanity–as they judged them–but unlike her, he hated it and hated himself for having to do it.

Since becoming a vampire, a strange type of loneliness had worked its way around her love for him. She hadn't noticed how it threatened to consume her until the possibility arose that there was someone out there who understood what it was like to be a woman in her situation. And maybe it was someone who got the same thrill that she did from the hunt.

She dressed in black leggings, a red button-down blouse, and black flats. The night was cool, so she added an oversized black blazer. Nice, but not too constricting if things went sideways.

It occurred to her that Adam would probably have been supportive of her quest for a new friend but that was a risk Cara was unwilling to take. A few deep breaths at the door did not assuage her guilt, nor did they dampen her resolve; so, she turned her full attention to the feminist vampire from the city and tossed her purse onto the passenger seat of her sedan.

The unofficial speed limit on Arizona highways was five over and the Highway Patrol probably wouldn't waste their time for anything under ten, but Cara was testing them that night. She hit the I-10 out of Chuparosa at about eighty-five on her way to Phoenix, much like she'd done decades earlier as an independent young woman leaving the safety of her small town to live on her own for the first time.

Cara's pulse quickened when she spotted the red Ford in front of the coffee shop and she parked in the space right next to it, resisting the urge to try one of its door handles. Since the vampire woman had emerged from the alley to show herself before, Cara started her search behind the shop, picking her way between the dumpsters and the flattened cardboard boxes to the back of the movie theater at the end of the strip mall.

After encountering enough rats and roaches to ruin her appetite for days, she retraced her steps until the stench abated and the alley spit her back out to the parking lot. Still no vampires. At that point she finally allowed herself to take a peek in the truck window.

It was pristine. There were no papers, no trash, no dash mat, nothing hanging from the review mirror, no decoration at all except for a National Rifle Association sticker on the glove box. Not that she was one to generalize, but the sticker and the license plate just didn't give off the same vibe as the lavender haired feminist. Of course, it could belong to someone she knew, but Cara had a feeling the truck was stolen.

She began to feel stupid and vulnerable, and scanned the parking lot for danger. Had she expected the other vampire to approach her with some kind of 'welcome to the Arizona chapter of the blood suckers club' gift basket? One that contained stemless wine glasses painted with little white fangs and a ceremonial rolodex filled with the addresses of local rapists for her to hunt?

The truth was that though they had *some* scruples, she and Adam were essentially cold-blooded killers, and there was no reason to believe that other vampires would have anything like their code of conduct. She decided to get her bearings and a cup of coffee before heading back to Chuparosa.

Once home, she would tell Adam everything so they could figure out the mystery together. She could even open up to him about how she'd been feeling. It was possible that there was a time when he felt the same way.

Cara stopped short in the doorway of the coffee shop and the hair stood up on her arms. The lavender haired vampire sat alone at a table by the window, wiggling her fingers to say 'hello'.

The vampire must have been watching her for a while and Cara was annoyed by that. She shoved the long door handle and stomped over to her table.

"Who are you?" she demanded.

Lavender hair smiled and handed her a tiny paper cup. "Double espresso, right?"

How long had she been watching her? Cara took the cup and stuck out her hand.

"I assume you know my name."

Lavender hair lowered her eyelids and whispered, "Busted," and after ignoring Cara's extended hand for an uncomfortable moment, she gave the tips of her fingers a little shake and said, "Betty."

Cara eyed the espresso and set it on the table. "No thanks."

"Good girl." Betty gave her a devlish smirk. "I've been waiting for you."

"How did you know I'd show up tonight?"

Betty shrugged. "Just a hunch." A hunch that became more of an educated guess after one of her secret trips to Chuparosa when she spied the men leaving with their fishing gear.

Betty appeared to be somewhere in her early forties, but Cara knew that meant nothing, she could have lived for thousands of years. She had hazel eyes and a button nose, and she had probably been an adorable child but, while pretty, she'd grown into a rather average woman. Cara supposed that she dyed her hair so brightly to stand out. She wore jeans again but with a solid black sweatshirt and black cross trainers. Her straight locks were pulled into a short ponytail at the nape of her neck.

"Are you expecting trouble tonight?" Cara asked.

"Not with you."

Cara raised an eyebrow, looking around at the Saturday coffee shop crowd on their laptops, laughing with their friends.

"I'm going on a rescue mission," Betty explained. "There's an empty warehouse downtown that's being used to process girls that were brought up from Mexico."

Cara shook her head. "I think that's just a rumor."

"Well, I think it's true." Betty's face hardened. "I won't be the one who lets them suffer. Do you know what they do to those girls?"

Cara did know, and it filled her with rage. The Super Bowl was coming to Glendale soon and there would be an unprecedented demand for girls. She'd planned to check it out the other night, and supposed it was worth following up even if it turned out to be nothing, as she guessed it would be.

Chapter Six

Two blocks from the warehouse on East Buckeye Road, Cara pulled in behind the red truck. With every warning bell in her brain going off at once, she followed as Betty led them around to the back. They peered into the warehouse from the side of a filthy, twelve-foot moving truck parked in front of an open steel hinged door. The smell of vanilla wafted through the air and Cara could not tell where the unsettling juxtaposition was coming from.

One man who looked to be somewhere in his twenties pulled a strip of packing tape across the top of a large cardboard box and then called out for help from another man who appeared to be about the same age. Betty and Cara retreated into the darkness while they loaded the box on the truck and when they went back inside, Cara whispered, "This is not a trafficking situation."

Betty tapped her shoulder and nodded toward an old steel desk at the other end of the room. "There's a girl."

There was a girl in her late teens sitting on top of the desk, laughing and shooting staples at the second man as he walked by. A cloud hung over her and Cara realized then that the vanilla scent was coming from a vape pen the girl held in her other hand.

Even if there was a warehouse full of girls, Cara knew that wasn't it. Those men had probably stolen the stuff in the boxes, but the girl on the desk wasn't a captive. If anything, she was flirting with one of them.

She glared at Betty and said, "I'm leaving."

Betty shoved her against the warehouse, making a crash against the aluminum that they were sure to have heard inside.

"What are you doing?" Cara struggled against the other woman, not used to an adversary who possessed strength equal to her own. "They're not hurting her."

"So naïve." Betty released her and resecured her ponytail, then walked through the open door calling over her shoulder, "I promise you they've hurt someone else."

Her mind raced but before she could even fathom Betty's mindset, one of the young men hollered, "What the hell?"

"Shit." She ran inside to find the girl cowering behind the first man as Betty lifted the second man, his face swollen from a blow, by the shirt. Tiny Betty extended her arm all the way over her head to get him off his feet.

"What are you doing?" Cara shouted.

Betty ignored her and brought the man close. His eyes widened as she lowered her fangs and then he gasped when in one swift movement, she pulled him to her and sank her teeth into his neck.

"Terry!" The girl screamed.

The first man roughly pushed the girl behind the desk where she crouched with her hands over her ears, whimpering Terry's name over and over.

He sprinted out and returned with a lug wrench, but Cara held him back.

"Take the girl and get out of here," she warned, "or that woman will kill you."

His eyes darted from her to where Betty drained Terry's twitching body, then he took a step back and swung the wrench at Cara. She snatched it out of his hand and grabbed him by the scruff of the neck, using just enough force to incapacitate him as she bounced his head off the desk.

He collapsed unconscious and Cara ordered the girl to run, but as she scrambled from behind the desk, Betty tossed the lifeless Terry aside and grabbed the teenager by throat. The color drained from the girl's face, and she made a sick gurgling noise as Betty choked her to death.

"Enough!" Cara screamed.

She lunged to stop her, but there was no mistaking the gruesome crunch as the girl's cervical spine splintered in Betty's grip.

Betty's expression then darkened so dramatically that Cara stopped short.

"The young ones are so lucky," she said dreamily, stroking the girl's cheek as her head flopped over, "look at that smooth skin." She shoved the body at Cara, who pressed her hands to her mouth in disbelief.

"You're crazy," she whispered.

Betty's eyes were wild as she licked the blood from her fangs. "You have no idea."

Cara flew at her but at the sound of a whistle from outside, Betty dropped the girl and sprinted out of the metal doors. Cara followed but again stopped short, this time at the sight of the narrow pink strip of color on the horizon.

"Oh my god."

She ran to her car where a stout man with shoulder length, wavy, ash blonde hair leaned against the driver's side door. She thought at first that he might be unsheltered, but if that were the case he was very well dressed in black jeans, motorcycle boots and a tan leather vest over a long-sleeved white Henley. What really struck her were the red, splotchy blisters around his eyes.

"What's your hurry, blondie?" he asked.

His British accent was so thick that she barely understood his words. She pushed him aside, never taking her eyes off the widening pink strip of light over the warehouse.

"Okay, okay." He laughed and spit tobacco near her front tire as she got in and locked the doors.

Cara sped away thinking that he was lucky it was her car and not the Ford that he'd chosen to lean against that morning. She cast a glance at the passenger seat and couldn't believe her purse and phone were still there. Her stomach dropped though when she saw that there were five text messages and three missed calls from Adam.

With the deadly sunrise in her rearview mirror, she once again tested the limits of the Highway Patrol as she raced back to Chuparosa. Tears filled her eyes as she contemplated being burned alive, and she'd never been so afraid.

* * *

Adam had kept himself glued to the window to watch for her, and he threw open the front door as she finally screeched up to the house.

"Stop!" She shouted to keep him from racing outside to help her. The sunrise was complete and though she'd parked as close as she could, she would surely get burned on her way in.

He ignored her, pulled up the hood of his sweatshirt, stretched the sleeves over his hands, and sprinted to her side. As he guided her up the walkway, she held the blazer over her head for cover, screaming as the sun scorched the exposed skin on her hands. In the short time it took to get inside, painful sores bubbled all the way to her wrists.

"God, Cara where were you?" Adam ran cold water in the kitchen sink and plunged her hands in the stream. "What is happening?"

The pain and the fear and the shock from the night's events had her so tongue-tied all she could do was stare at her hands in the water and shake her head.

He thought of Sam's silent threat and took her by the shoulders, turning her to face him. "Are you trying to get yourself killed? Is that what you want?

"Adam...please." After everything else, the pain in his eyes, the pain she'd caused, was too much for her to bear.

"Talk to me, god dammit," he raised his voice in desperation, "talk to me!"

Her hands were already healing with a delicate new layer of skin forming over the burns, but they trembled as she reached for him. "I'm sorry. I can't. Not now."

He could not believe it. Jerking away from her, he stormed into the bedroom, slamming the door behind him. Twice he put his hand on the doorknob to go to her but in the end just sat on the edge of the bed with his head in his hands.

While his heart broke, she slumped in a chair at the kitchen table and sobbed. She couldn't imagine why, but she'd been set up, and Cara was determined not to bring the Betty problem down on him.

Before he turned her, Adam was quite explicit about all the ways in which vampires could be killed, so she knew exactly what to do when she found Betty. By sunset she had made a decision that would affect nearly everyone she cared about.

Fresh tears streamed down her face as she wrote him a note:

Adam, there's something I have to finish. Let me do this alone and I promise I'll never leave without you again. I love you, and I am yours forever. Cara

Chapter Seven

Adam read Cara's note at least a hundred times before his disbelief gave way to acceptance. Even then, he looked out the window in case her car just happened to pull in. Worry and heartache overtook him and he crumpled the paper, absently letting it fall from his hands. Though she promised to return, she didn't say when and the suffocating silence in the house reminded him of how it had been before she came to live with him. He didn't know if he could stand it, even if only for a little while.

"Come on Carl." He zipped on a hoodie, grabbed his backpack, and strode down the street in a mental fog. The dog stiffened when they came upon Sebastian Scott's house because Carl knew that Watson, a massive German Shepherd, lived there. Though the dogs had done battle side by side, Carl was always on his guard around the former hellhound.

Adam slowed and ducked behind a Mesquite tree. Subconsciously, he'd been seeking out his friend, but he had second thoughts when Laura appeared with Bash on the porch. It was a cool January night, but she wore nothing but thick fuzzy socks and one of Bash's flannel shirts. Cara never wore Adam's clothes and he laughed to himself trying to imagine her in anything flannel, ever.

A possessive part of him suddenly wished more than anything that Cara *would* wear one of his shirts. He wondered if Bash ever indulged in that sort of cave man satisfaction, or if he simply thought it was sexy as hell.

They'd just made love—Adam could smell it on them. He didn't begrudge the couple one single second of their hard-won happiness, but his chest burned with jealousy. Laura's green eyes sparkled when she looked at Bash and she sank into his arms when he reached for her from the oversized chaise lounge. They'd been picking through a tray of snacks on the bistro table and were each holding mugs of hot chocolate spiked with so much Bailey's Irish Cream that you didn't need to be a vampire to catch the scent from his distance.

Bash twirled a finger around one of Laura's long copper-colored curls and when he bent his head to kiss her neck, Adam took the opportunity to cross the street. His hopes of escaping unseen were dashed though, when he heard Laura call out, "Were you just going to pass us by without saying hello?"

Adam stuffed his hands in his pockets and shuffled up the walkway. "I didn't want to intrude."

"Whatever," she scoffed, "have some hot chocolate with us."

"Oh, no," he protested, "Laura that's not—"

But she'd already disappeared into the house, so he gave Bash a guilty shrug. His friend's eyes were glassy from the liquor, but they bore into him as if he knew that something was amiss. Still, his tone was light, and he chuckled at Adam's third wheel discomfort.

"Have a seat," he gestured to one of the bistro chairs, "she's never gonna let you leave."

Adam flipped a chair around and straddled it, resting his arms on the back. "Actually, I was hoping you could tell me where Drew is," he lied. "I could have called him, but it's such a nice night, I thought..." His voice trailed off as he realized that, though he had the grace to ignore it, Bash knew that he was full of shit. Everyone in town was aware that Pastor Andrew Clarke ran the Al-Anon meetings at the YMCA on Sunday nights.

Fortunately, Laura returned with a steaming mug of hot chocolate for Adam and some peanut butter treats for Carl and Watson before things got even more uncomfortable between the two men. Bash busied himself by giving the dogs their snacks but kept a side-eye on Adam the whole time.

He inhaled over the top of the mug and the tension in his back visibly eased before he even took his first sip. Though Bash was on to him, or perhaps because of that, Adam felt safe on the porch in their company. Sharing their delicious hot chocolate was the first real comfort he'd known all day.

"You good?" Bash finally asked.

It was a miracle that they let him near their house at all, let alone call him their friend, but Adam had worked hard to win their trust. It was no small feat, considering Bash's prior experience with vampires was the near-death kind. Then Adam had turned Cara, who was one of Laura's closest friends. Despite Cara's insistence that the choice to do it was hers alone, Laura was a powerful witch who could have made him suffer for it on principle.

If Laura knew where Cara was, she hid it well that night, though he would have been surprised if Cara had taken such a risk by telling her. As well, *he* would not put Bash and Laura in any more danger than they routinely put themselves in by bringing it up.

In Daniel's absence they had to lead Heaven's Watch, and he didn't want them to worry about other vampires who might or might not be lurking around, or even about Cara running off. The thought of his maker being in Chuparosa sent a shiver down his spine, but he would find out for sure before he brought them into his problems. It occurred to him then that perhaps Cara was safer wherever she was.

"I've had better days," Adam said finally, "but I'm fine." Adam's life was falling apart, but a pang of guilt shot through him for at least he was still upright. "How's Chuck?"

The barbs in the tongue of the Chersydros had released a toxin into Chuck for which there was no antidote. As long as his heart held out, the doctor assured them that the poison would make its way through his system, but there was no way of knowing how much damage would be left behind.

"Still pretty sick," Bash said. "We just have to give him some time." After all they'd been through, he refused to consider the gruesome possibility. Bash always knew that something horrible would take him out, and he'd long since made peace with that certainty, but being spared to mourn the loss of his friends was unthinkable.

Adam gave him a solemn nod, stood and kissed

Laura's hand. "Thanks for everything, beautiful. I should go if I'm gonna catch Drew. I need to talk some shop with him."

Drew was a preacher by calling but, like Adam, an electrician by trade. So, while his story was plausible, Bash had been a cop his entire adult life and he didn't like the demoralized look in Adam's eyes.

If there was one thing Chuparosa substance abuse meetings were not, it was anonymous. In such a small town, few who attended could expect the others in the circle to respect their privacy. That they were there in the first place indicated that circumstances were dire enough to warrant the certainty of everyone being in their business.

Pastor Clarke was known for his helpful resources, and for always knowing exactly what to say, but what Adam observed was that Drew said very little during the meeting. Leaning forward with his elbows on his knees, he listened intently with a non-judgmental ear, creating an atmosphere of safety and hope in the harshly lit community room.

Soaking up the energy of the place, Adam stayed out of sight near the back until Drew began to wrap things up, ducking away when the group bowed their heads. He decided to confide in his friends when the timing was better and, instead of confronting his empty house, opted to spend the remaining dark hours with a more captive audience.

He sent Cara a text that read: `I'm here if you need me` and made his way through the darkness.

The screech of the rusty push bar interrupted

Drew's closing prayer and he looked up in time to see Adam's unmistakable silhouette slipping out the heavy back door. Adam was not an extraordinarily tall man, and though he had the lean muscular build of someone who'd worked hard in the outdoors all his life, there was an ethereal quality to his movements that reminded Drew of the angels.

As usual when the meeting dispersed, Drew was headed to Isaac's Oasis for a beer when he caught sight of Adam in the murky light around the library and decided to follow. Adam unknowingly led him through the residential area and into the open desert where he hesitated for a moment, trying to guess the vampire's destination.

As he continued on, the outline of a cowboy hat appeared on the ground to his left and a hand grabbed his shoulder from behind.

"Jesus Christ!" He was so startled that he just knew several of his precious few remaining years had fallen away.

Bash stood in front of him with a finger to his lips. "Shhh."

Drew put a hand to his chest, attempting to whisper as he gasped, "Where'd you come from?"

"The question is: where's he going?" Bash nodded in Adam's direction.

"I was trying to figure that out before you scared the shit out of me."

"Sorry," Bash smirked, "sort of."

They watched Adam for a while longer and then Drew said, "Looks like he's going up."

When they reached the trail at the bottom of Shock Butte, Bash slapped him on the back. "After you."

Drew held back, muttering, "I don't think so," and with a chuckle Bash took the lead.

51

Chapter Eight

"Me again." Adam tossed his backpack against the stone marking Daniel's grave. "No, no, don't get up."

He laughed to himself at his terrible joke and took another swig from the whiskey bottle. He'd grown more despondent on the way up the butte and began to think back on the few times he himself had been singed by the sun. If he just sat next to Daniel until morning, would he explode into flames, or would he be slowly blistered to death?

Both options terrified him and in truth, no matter how bad things had gotten over the years, he was never suicidal. But he was tired. Deep down he knew that his wish for a quieter life in Chuparosa was never going to come true.

He'd placed his hopes in the love of a woman who accepted her powers on the understanding that she be allowed to use them. Of course, Cara's determination and strength were a huge part of why he loved her but...damn. *So tired.*

Bash and Drew shared a knowing look when they

reached the top of the butte. One of Adam's arms hung straight at his side with the whiskey bottle in his hand and he held the other out to steady himself as his body swayed under the influence of the alcohol. Unaware of them, he teetered on the east rim, gazing at the town below.

Carl growled low at the Bobs, who circled him curiously, making sure they used caution as they did so. The dog looked from Bash and Drew to Adam and the bobcats and back as if to say, "Can you give me a hand here?"

"Adam," Drew's voice was calm but commanding, "get away from the edge."

Adam's back stiffened and when he turned around his shoulders sank with shame. "Shit."

"We've all been there." Bash shrugged.

"Why did you follow me?"

Drew reached out and nudged him away from the rim, saying, "Give us a little credit, alright? We're your friends."

"As it turns out," Adam waved a finger at them, "that may not be in your best interest after all."

"We'll be the judge of that after you tell us what's going on."

"Where do I even start?" Adam furrowed his brow, frustrated by his muddled state of mind and glaring at the bottle in his hand. "You would think after all this time, I'd remember that this doesn't help."

He stumbled backward a bit as he wound up, but still managed to pitch the bottle into the center of the rock formation, sending the Bobs scrambling away when it shattered.

As they stood waiting for Adam to find the right

words, the cool night air turned icy around them, and a thin layer of frost covered everything in sight.

They noticed that the rustling of the rodents in the bushes had stilled and that even the incessant buzz of insects had ceased. The butte quieted in anticipation of something the men were quite sure they wanted no part of, yet they could not summon the will to leave. Exhaling their foggy breath, they exchanged weary glances as the outline of the whiskey on the rock began to glow.

The liquid caught fire, creating a blue ring of flames from which stepped a being they recognized instantly though they'd never laid eyes on him before. For a few moments the oxygen was sucked out of the air and the men fell to their knees grasping at their throats.

Lucifer appeared to them as a clean-cut middle aged man wearing jeans, loafers, and a navy-blue cardigan over a crisp white t-shirt. He took a knee and ran his fingers through Drew's hair, smiling as the preacher writhed away.

"Alright," he waived his hand over them, "go ahead and breathe."

At once they inhaled sharp gulps of air and, as their lungs filled and their color returned, they crawled to one another, closing ranks.

Lucifer slid his hands into his pockets and rocked back on his heels. "I assume no introductions are necessary."

"What does the Devil want with us?" Bash choked.

"The nearer men are to God, the more susceptible they are to—"

"Then like I said," Bash cut him off, "why are you bothering with *us?*"

"There are many devils in Hell, Sebastian, trapped for eternity, one hopes. Angels, however, are free to go where they choose. Angels are with you all the time. Even me."

He took off his sweater, laid it across Daniel's headstone, and then a baseball cap materialized in his hand. He put it on backward over his mop of black hair and squatted in front of them. He winked at Bash, who realized with a start that he was looking at the coroner's assistant he'd met briefly at the lake.

"We can be anyone or no one," Lucifer confirmed, "some of us will guard you, some will spy on you and, if you ask nicely, some of us will even advise you."

"But," Adam swallowed hard, "what do *you* do?"

"I provide knowledge. It is...my only crime."

The bitterness in his tone did not go unnoticed and it made the men so uneasy that they scooted even closer together.

"Knowledge is power," he added, "and I, unlike some, am all about empowerment."

That explains why he looks like a college professor. Drew thought. Though his appearance was average and unassuming, something inside of each man found Lucifer so exquisite that it gave them uncomfortable thoughts. Drew studied the angel, captivated by the grace in his movements and the main feature he shared with others of his kind: piercing dark crystal blue eyes that Drew dared not meet with his own. *A college professor who demands sex for good grades.*

"That power isn't necessarily used for good," Drew countered.

Lucifer shrugged. "Good and evil are matters of perspective."

Bash used Daniel's tombstone to steady himself as he stood up, then reached out to haul the others to their feet. "If you're all about sharing knowledge," he demanded, "then answer my question."

"Hell is home to a collection of the old gods." Lucifer pulled on his sweater and the baseball cap disappeared. "Some have been there for so long that their children's children are now my prisoners. Like you, they did not ask to be born and they resent their fate."

Bash sighed but chose not to argue the oversimplification of his circumstances. "I thought Hell was reserved for humans after we die."

"There are humans in Hell, but I assure you they were not dead when they got there."

Bash also decided to let that horrifying comment slide. "These old gods...anyone in particular we should be concerned about?"

"Your race is charging headlong into its own destruction, but not quickly enough for one of those children I mentioned." Lucifer lifted the leather cord around Drew's neck and stroked the wooden crucifix at his throat. "Lovely," he purred and then took Drew's hand and dropped a small scroll in his palm.

Drew shook off the unpleasant feeling in his stomach and unfurled it to find a symbol and a name. "Bellinor Díoltas." He read, and then handed the scroll to Bash.

"Why didn't Thomas tell us about this?"

"Thomas?" Lucifer cracked his knuckles while repeating the fallen angel's name. "Thomas's seeming redemption has given hope to his race but those Watchers who remain in Hell don't know that he's only allowed to live because of you. If he returns for any reason, he will be pulled apart molecule by molecule over centuries. I will see to it myself."

"Then why are you helping us?" Adam asked.

"Make no mistake about this: I only concern myself with your mission because I want to go home, and I cannot do that if Earth falls to the forces that would overtake her."

Lucifer grabbed Adam by the throat and before the others could react, four skeletal demons raced out of the fiery portal in the rock to restrain them. Long red fingers burned into their skin like branding irons as they struggled to get away.

"Get your house in order," Lucifer hissed in Adam's ear, "before your affairs bleed into the work of the Watch." He lifted him off the ground, warning, "You'd better sort the clowns from the lion tamers in this circus before it's too late." Their closeness caused Adam's stomach to heave bile into his throat as Lucifer pulled them chest to chest. "Give the lion tamers the trust they deserve," he commanded, "or all of us will lose everything."

A shadow crossed Lucifer's face just then and they caught a flash of what might have been worry in his eyes before he continued, "As the veil thins, not only do the persecuted ones work to rid this planet of humans, they also seek revenge on the god who sentenced them to their suffering. While you must destroy your maker, Adam Colter, I will stop at nothing to protect mine."

He released Adam, shoving him toward his friends and waving the demons away.

"Alright," Drew sat back on his heels gaping at the thin tendrils of smoke rising from his seared skin, "you've made your point. Of course, we're gonna help

Adam get his shit together, but you've got to tell us what you know about this Bellinor guy's plan."

Lucifer gave them a crooked smile and said, "I know that Bellinor is a female."

"If she's in Hell, why don't you deal with her?" Adam asked.

"As you know, angels have singular purpose. Humans are the ones with all the potential for greatness."

"That's just fabulous." Bash plucked his cowboy hat out of the dirt, slapped it on his thigh and put it back on his head. "There's an angry woman from Hell comin' after us and you have no idea when, how or where."

"I will do my part and find out. In the meantime," he leveled his gaze onto Adam, "you will do what you must to prepare."

"Why should we trust you?"

Lucifer thought for a moment. "Your friend from the lake is dying," he said.

"No," Bash shook his head, "Chuck will be alright. He just needs time."

Compassion filled Lucifer's voice. "Sebastian, your friend is dying. But I will see what I can do about that."

Then the darkest of angels turned his back to them and disappeared into the rock, leaving only the moonlight behind as the flames died away.

They were silent for a while until, his chest tightening, Drew said, "Why do I get the feeling that we just made a deal?"

Chapter Nine

Cara was careful not to look in the review mirror as she drove away from Chuparosa that night. If all went well, she would be back in a couple of days, and she'd have a new friend with her. Her old friends would take some convincing of course, and they wouldn't be wrong to doubt her. Betty had some serious issues but, didn't they all? They were witches and vampires for Christ's sake and none of them were innocent, not even when they were kids.

After Cara thought it through, she realized that Betty was more like her than she had previously been willing to admit. What if, instead of fighting they could find some common ground? Cara still craved the companionship of a woman who could understand her lifestyle and stubbornly clung to the idea that Betty would be the one.

Adam would be harder to convince. She would never forget the look on his face as he ran the cool water over her burning hands, and it would be difficult to earn back his trust. She liked to think that they had plenty of time for that, but it wouldn't matter if in the end he decided that loving her had been a mistake.

If he meant it, something he said when he made her a vampire inspired a thread of assurance for their future.

While they made love on that night, he pressed in on the sides of her throat with his fingers and, as her vision blurred, he lowered his fangs and waited. At the height of her climax, he sank his teeth into her neck, sucking her blood in rhythm to the slow deep thrust of his hips. When her head lolled back on the pillow, he took a pocketknife from the nightstand and, after making a cut over his collar bone, placed her lips to it and rolled her on top of him.

His blood had the sweet, spicy taste of cloves and as she drank from him, his hands played over every inch of her body, which she was becoming more and more aware of as her strength returned. The breeze from the ceiling fan was like an icy blast on her damp skin and she noticed as she pressed up to ride him that she could see through the darkness as if it were nothing but a thin veil over her eyes.

Adam softly talked her through the changes so she wouldn't be afraid, but everything about the experience excited her and she felt no fear. When she tensed again, he roughly rolled her underneath him, thrusting harder and faster until she screamed his name. They came together in wave after wave of a visceral pleasure the likes of which she had never felt before or since.

He'd collapsed on top of her and nuzzled the bitten place on her neck, whispering, "No matter what happens between us, I will never abandon you to this life."

He'd expected it to take months or even years for

her to adjust but, with his support, the difficulties she experienced during her first tentative steps into his world were surprisingly short-lived. She felt no shame over the biological requirements of her new life but, somehow, hurting Adam had become as easy as killing bad guys and for that she did hate herself.

The cell phone ring jolted her thoughts back to the present and she looked down at the name of the caller with relief. A client of hers was a retired private investigator and she'd asked him to run the R3DN3K license plate on Betty's truck. He found her a name and the address of a small house in the Encanto neighborhood just outside of downtown Phoenix. Though Justin Eggers hadn't reported it, the truck had likely been stolen from him and he might have caught a glimpse of the thief. It was a start.

Feeling no need to hide her presence, Cara parked out front and strolled up to the door. The house was older, a cute refurbished two bedroom—the kind rich urban pioneers liked to flip, driving the prices up and the locals out. There were no other cars in the driveway, so she wasn't surprised when her knock went unanswered.

She snuck a peek through the slats of the blinds in the front window and her heart sank. The remnants of a violent struggle littered the living room and there was no sign of Justin. After the handle crushed in her grip, the front door swung open and she let herself in, righting an upended couch that blocked the entryway.

Broken glass crunched under her every step as she worked her way around a smashed coffee table and the contents of a bookshelf that had been yanked away from the wall.

Several open Styrofoam containers of half-eaten take-out Mexican food were left on the kitchen counter along with at least a dozen empty beer bottles. Her pulse quickened as she thought, *Betty isn't alone.* A wide trail of blood smeared along the tile led her to one of the bedrooms, but she could have just followed the smell of decomposition down the hall.

All hopes of making a friend in Betty dissolved as she entered the room and found that Justin's mutilated body had been flung so hard against the wall that he'd nearly gone through the closet into the bathroom. She stared at him for a long time while trying to process the scene. It was gruesome but she was more perplexed than squeamish. Somehow, Justin seemed to have an extra foot, but when she pulled on what remained of the closet door, a dead woman who had been stuffed next to him fell out at her feet.

Her fists balled up at her sides and she stalked to the back of the house. When satisfied there were no more bodies, she ran through a mental list of all the ways Adam had warned that she could die. Vampires could be weakened and even badly hurt, but Betty would have to be incinerated with sunlight, staked with wood, poisoned, or separated from her head.

Cara had killed a lot of men since becoming a vampire, and she'd come up with plenty of inventive ideas to do it quickly, if not painlessly; but she'd never killed one of her own kind. She picked up a coffee table leg, splintered it against the counter and reminded herself that Betty could be planning the same thing.

She heard the truck pull in the driveway and moved

out of the light. Betty would have seen her car and could probably sense her presence so there was no point in trying to hide, but Cara hoped for at least some element of surprise.

Betty paused at the threshold of the front door and called out with a cheerful, "Helloooo!"

As Cara suspected, she wasn't alone. She waved in two regular guys who split up to search the house and then closed the door behind her. The first guy went down the hall to the bedrooms and the second guy backed directly into Cara's chest. He was much bigger than her, but she was stronger, and he bellowed out as she twisted his arms behind his back. Betty whirled around and Cara moved the man with her into the light.

"There you are!" She clapped her hands with joy. "I told him you'd be here, and I *knew* you wouldn't let me down."

Cara thought that, for a second, Betty really did look relieved to see her, but the guy distracted her by trying to wrestle away. She shoved him down to his knees, slamming his head against the wall and, when he fell unconscious, she picked up the table leg and twirled it in her hand.

"This ends now," she said, and ran at her.

Betty caught Cara's arm before it came down with the makeshift stake and kneed her in the stomach. Cara doubled over but held tight to the table leg and came up swinging it like a baseball bat, hitting Betty squarely under the chin. She flew backward and when the stake split apart, Cara charged at her again with both pieces. Before she could stab her, another man rushed through the front door and tackled Cara to the couch.

The new man was a vampire and, under the strength

of his attack, the couch slid across the room and crashed into the kitchen island. Cara scrambled out from underneath him but found herself backed against the counter.

"Uh oh," Betty sang out, "daddy's home." She gathered herself and slunk behind the kitchen island.

The man said, "Hey blondie," and spit tobacco on what Cara estimated was an eleven-hundred-dollar area rug under his feet. Not that anything could ever be salvaged from that house. "Little B was right. You saved me a lot of trouble by coming here on your own."

Cara looked at Betty, who was beaming with pride. Then she turned back and studied the man in front of her before gasping with recognition. He was the one leaning on her car outside of the warehouse in Glendale the night Betty killed those kids.

"Getting you away from that man of yours was easier than I thought it would be," he said. "Is there trouble in paradise?"

Cara caught that British accent again and her heart jumped into her throat.

Her voice shook as she said, "I think you know his name."

"That I do. Mr. Colter and I go way back." He moved the tobacco to the other side of his mouth and spit again.

"Oh my god," *no wonder Adam had been acting so strangely,* "you're Walter Sallow." *Why didn't he tell me Walter was in town?*

The second guy emerged from the hallway and posted himself next to Walter. He had bite marks all over him, but like the one she knocked out, he wasn't a vampire–they'd only been feeding on him. Cara curled her lip and started to speak but then two gun shots rang out from behind her and the guy next to Walter crumpled in front of them.

She stared at Walter, baffled by his laughter, and then she felt the pain. Panic set in when she looked down at the two exit wounds in her chest, finally grasping the fact that the bullets had gone through her and into Walter's strongman. She pressed frantically at the wounds with her hands and just before the room went dark, she saw that Betty still held out the pistol she'd used to shoot her in the back.

Chapter Ten

"Charming? Lucifer? Lucifer was...charming?" Laura found it more and more difficult to keep the hysteria out of her voice as she rummaged through their sizable first aid kit for burn ointment.

Adam's breath caught in his throat as Bash's flannel shirt rode up when she reached for the kit in the cabinet. He then noted with relief that she'd put on a pair of red fleece pajama shorts under it. Not that she was likely to hang around half-naked in front of them, but after their encounter on the porch, his mental state was too fragile to have his lovely friend exposed to him.

"Charming in a Ted Bundy sort of way," Drew tried to explain.

"Good god." A chill had settled deep in her spine since the men had shown up fifteen minutes earlier with their blistered skin and impossible story.

As a witch, not to mention the daughter of a fallen angel, she'd been threatened with Lucifer for her entire life. Her father had only recently escaped from Hell after centuries of imprisonment and her own existence was an affront to the many other beings who had a say in her future. There were too many, in fact. The unfairness of that filled her with resentment, which was suddenly tempered by the terrible certainty of the Devil so close on her heels. He was finally part of their lives. For real.

She narrowed her eyes at the thought of her father. "Where was Thomas during all of this?"

"That's a great question." Drew shrugged. "I wouldn't make any sudden moves if I were him. Lucifer is not a fan."

"Fabulous."

Bash took Laura's hands in his and met her eyes. "You and your sister have got to be careful, baby." He could only imagine what the implications would be, should Lucifer ever make contact with one of them.

All three men shifted uncomfortably. They'd been wondering the same thing: could they stop him if Lucifer wanted to use the power within the angel witches for himself? Unwilling to dwell on that, Bash gave her a squeeze, adding, "We'll worry about him later, okay."

"Worry about your deal with the Devil later?"

"He's technically an angel, not a devil," Drew corrected.

"Noted." She made a face and turned on the faucet to wash her hands. Nodding to the kitchen island, she said, "Sit down and let me take care of you."

Bash and Drew did as instructed, shrugging out of their shirts and easing onto a couple of tall stools.

Laura conceded that Bash had a point. If what the men said was true, Lucifer and his assignment were still something of a future problem. So she vowed to keep everyone's spirits up, at least until they could get Adam to confide in them. Anything Lucifer had to say would be irrelevant if they couldn't survive what the vampire had been hiding.

As gentle as she tried to be, Drew paled as she treated his wounds. "You know," she fluttered her lashes at him, "I love being able to massage all these big muscles, but you guys give me the worst reasons why."

Drew blushed and then Bash stole a kiss as she washed her hands again and fished some nonstick gauze pads out of the kit.

"Here, Adam," she said, handing him one, "would you mind?"

"Alright, but I'm not kissing you," he said as he placed the pad over Drew's burn.

"What? I thought you had a thing for blondes." Drew laughed, then winced as Adam pressed it into place.

"I like mine a lot shorter," Adam said, sadness shining in his eyes at the thought of Cara.

Laura finished bandaging Bash and while they put their shirts back on, she rested her hand on Adam's arm. He covered it with his own and braced himself for the difficult question he knew was coming.

"Where is Cara?" She asked softly.

"If I knew, I'd be with her." He searched Laura's face for some sign of secret female information. Seeing nothing but concern, his shoulders sagged, and he told them how she left him.

As they listened, Bash and Drew softened their faces with sympathetic expressions, unable to imagine their lives without Laura and Sarah.

However, Laura's gaze turned stony, her thoughts

imperceptible to him. Adam couldn't tell if she was just trying to take it all in or if she blamed him for letting Cara go. What he didn't know is that she was angry with Cara, not him. Her impetuous behavior had been the cause of unnecessary headaches on many occasions, but this time she hadn't even let Laura in on her plans and that was beyond worrisome.

He took an uneasy breath before going on. "There's more," Adam said, "and it's not easy for me to talk about."

Laura flipped the kettle on to boil and went to the cabinet, selected a jar and measured three heaping spoons of its contents into a small cheesecloth pouch. After studying Adam for a second, she dropped in another scoop.

He went to the window and stood with his back to them, scanning the yard for danger. "It's possible that Cara is safer out there than we are here."

Bash shared a look with Drew and moved to fill the coffee pot with water. "We're listening."

Soon the air was filled with the rich aroma of brewing coffee but when Adam turned around, Laura set a mug of the tea she'd prepared in front of him.

"The last thing you need is caffeine. This will calm your nerves."

He frowned but didn't dare argue with her. Instead, he began his story, and did not spare them any of the details. For their own safety, they needed to know everything.

"When Lucifer told me to get my house in order, he was confirming what I'd suspected for a while: my maker is stalking me again and he may even be here in Chuparosa right now."

"When you say maker," Drew clarified, "do you mean the one who turned you into a vampire?"

Adam nodded and took a long sip of tea. Laura was right, his nerves settled and the more he talked, the more his inhibitions fell away.

"I killed Walter Sallow for the first time in 1864," Adam said, "but I did it wrong and that's how it all started."

He told them about how he met Jess, the vicious death of the boy's grandfather, and about the ensuing gunfight. He added that afterward, the sheriff had Walter buried in an unmarked grave just outside of town.

"What I didn't know then was that Walter was a vampire and when he told me to kill him, he meant *for good*." Adam rubbed his forehead. "I have no idea how I was supposed to know that, but he punched out of that grave so full of fury that he's spent over a hundred years seeking revenge on me."

"What happened to the boy?" Laura asked, horrified by the possibilities, "Jess was his name?"

"Yeah, Jess." Adam couldn't help but smile, remembering his friend. "We didn't know Walter was going to wake up so, after the burial, we found a doctor. His broken arm was infected, and I didn't think he was gonna make it." He shook his head. "But damn that kid was tough, and he pulled through." Adam chuckled, "I say kid, but I'd only just turned twenty myself."

"Babies!" Laura gasped, trying to imagine her twenty-one-year-old son on his own in the desert, getting into gunfights.

"I was a man by then–expected to be one anyway." He smiled again. "Jess regained most of his strength but—you'll appreciate this, Bash—he had to learn to be a southpaw for the rest of his life."

Bash laughed. "Then he was even tougher than I thought."

"Laura, Jess grew into, if not an altogether decent man," Adam gave her a wry look, "a damn good one, and the best friend I ever had. We rode together off and on for years, but he wasn't there when Walter finally caught up with me." He let out a long, slow breath. "For that I am so, so grateful."

"Will you tell us Adam?" Drew asked. "Tell us what happened to you."

"You know that I've been a lot of things in my life," Adam started, "but by the time I got to Bisbee, I was just plain tired." Adam closed his eyes and let the memories wash over him.

He knew that he was one of those devils Lucifer spoke of, just biding his time on earth, waiting to be locked up with all the others in Hell. No matter how hard he tried to block them out or how far he ran away, the devil's memories would forever haunt his every step.

Would Lucifer have mercy on him when some cruel thing eventually drove a stake through his heart, or when the hell of living finally drove him to walk into the sun? Would he be allowed to simply cease to exist or was there some new and worse nightmare waiting below?

He took another long sip of Laura's tea and opened his eyes to their expectant faces, realizing none of that mattered as long as he still had people to care about. There was no escaping the past, there were no answers to his questions, and his future was sure to be peppered with the loss of those who dared to love him. Would he lose the lion tamers who sat with him that night?

Lucifer advised him to give them the trust they deserved, so if they wanted to help rid him of Walter once and for all, he would let them. But first he had to relive it—the night he learned how to hate.

Chapter Eleven

As the full effect of Laura's potion began to hit him, he leaned back in his chair and attempted to travel back in time, to Bisbee, Arizona.

"I was a powderman and doing okay back then. I made three dollars and fifty cents a day blasting in the Copper Queen." He laughed at their expressions. "It was decent money at the time."

"I was getting too old to keep looking for trouble and I thought if I didn't blow himself up in the mine, I could make enough to buy a little place in the mountains–maybe even convince a certain someone to settle down with me."

He ignored the three sets of eyebrows that shot up and appreciated that they restrained themselves, letting him continue with only the pieces of the story he wanted to tell.

"Everyone was a little skittish the week it happened. Someone fell from a ladder, crushed a blasting cap and blew himself to smithereens. The incident had the miners rattled enough that a bunch of guys on my crew went to the saloon instead of work for several days."

Drew noticed that Adam's slight accent grew a bit stronger as he talked and what he'd suspected since they met appeared to be true. Adam mentioned to him once before that he was born in the United States, but at least one of his parents had to have been from Scotland.

"I woke up feeling poorly that day. In fact, I hadn't had much of an appetite for a few days, but me and Karl only had one more blast before the night crew came down. We'd just loaded the drill holes with dynamite and were cutting the fuses when a foul breeze came through the stope and snuffed out our candles.

"Dynamite by candlelight?" Bash was astonished. "Are you fucking kidding me?"

"Well," Adam chuckled, "safety wasn't of much concern to the boss men until later. Anyway, the Knockers started tapping in the timber, so you know we had to get out."

They'd once encountered the small, protective creatures known as Knockers while searching for Nick in an abandoned mine near Chuparosa. The others felt a bit closer to Adam just then, having experienced that part of his story for themselves.

"But it was the strangest thing: in the darkness, down the crosscut, I saw what looked like the embers of a cigar." He shook his head as if he still couldn't believe it. "No one, and I mean no one would have a lit cigar down there–the air was bad enough without those fumes. The Knockers went crazy then, banging like the whole thing was going to fall in. So, I lit a match to get my bearings, and grabbed Karl by the arm to make for the cage, but he but he wouldn't come with me. I was ready to punch him out and drag him away but then the cigar man's face hovered over us. He moved so fast and I...I could have sworn it was Walter. Walter who I killed all those years ago."

"He grabbed Karl by the throat, and I sprang at him, but he tossed me away like a rag doll. Karl yelled, 'get out of here!' but I just sat there in the dirt, stupefied. I watched Karl tilt his head up to the man, completely relaxed. I didn't know what to make of it all, so I did run and when I got to the cage, I looked back to see Walter bite down on Karl's neck."

Adam got up and paced the kitchen. His friends faded to the background of his sight, and he again found himself mentally walking the filthy streets he once called home.

Bisbee, Arizona - 1899

There was no one he could tell who wouldn't think he'd lost his mind, so he trudged up Brewery Gulch toward his boarding house, convincing himself they must have hit a pocket of poisonous gas that was causing hallucinations. Maybe it was the gas that had been making him sick all week.

Then he remembered that he'd never lit the fuses, so the powder never blew. He would have to report that to his supervisor, and by then his supervisor would be in the saloon.

After a quick stop at the bunkhouse for his pistol, he made his way past the Mercantile to the saloon, hoping that his supervisor was still standing. The stench of body odor, tobacco and rank beer brewed with rancid water wafted over him. Dry, hacking, consumptive coughs echoed through the place, nearly drowning out the fiddle player. Adam did not find his supervisor there, but Karl gave him a casual wave from the end of the bar.

Astonished, he pushed his way through the crowd to get to him and then froze in his tracks as Walter Sallow stepped between them. The skin around his eyes, pink and perpetually peeling, crinkled with amusement. Even then Adam could have told himself it wasn't Walter, but the desiccated wolf's ear still hung from the leather cord around his neck.

"Have a drink." Walter wasn't asking. He muscled Adam over to where Karl stood and ordered three whiskeys.

Karl was tall, skinny, and had even paler skin than most miners, but he looked particularly gaunt that night. Adam reached up and pulled the bandana away from his neck. Two bite marks pulsed, bloody and festering just above his collar bone. He leaned away with one hand on his pistol, resituating the cloth with his other.

"I killed you once," he said to Walter, "and I'll do it again if you don't tell me what's going on."

Walter turned his head and spit on the floor, splashing tobacco near Adam's boots. "You're not as good a shot as you think you are."

He tapped on his pistol grip and said, "I'm even better now than I was back then so, I'll ask you one more time, what are you?"

But Walter was gone. A woman screamed, several men teetered in his wake, and the doors swung wildly as he pushed through them with speed Adam couldn't even process.

He threw back his whiskey, which had been watered down with something vile, and glared at the bartender while ordering a beer. It wasn't likely to taste any better, but he hoped it would settle his churning stomach. The beer was cold and refreshing, but a wave of nausea followed it down his throat and a weakness overwhelmed him, buckling his knees. He leaned against the bar and looked up at Karl, gesturing at his neck.

"What has he done to you?"

"I give him blood and he takes care of me, but that's not what he has planned for tonight."

"What?" Adam covered his eyes with his hand in an effort to keep the room from spinning.

"Don't think about it now—you're getting sick too. Let's go." Karl took him by the arm and led him to the doors.

"Too?" Adam fell against him, still telling himself it was all because of a poisonous gas leak in the mine. "I'll be fine, I just need some air," he argued, but by the time they reached the bunkhouse, he was burning up with fever.

"Where is everyone?" The halls were empty and the only sounds they heard were the usual shots and shouts from the streets below, and Adam panting as he struggled to climb the stairs.

"Sick," Karl said, "like you."

"I'm not—" Adam caught a glimpse of himself in the scratched-up mirror over the wash basin and flinched at his reflection. A pattern of red spots peeked out of where his shirt opened at the collar. His hands trembled as he unbuttoned it all the way, revealing that his entire chest was covered in the rash.

It took him a minute more, but then it came together for him: the missing miners, the way he'd been feeling, the fever, the rash.

"No," he whispered, "no." He'd seen a Typhoid breakout once before, and it was a horrible way to die.

Karl eased him down to the thin, dirty mattress and he cried out, curling into a ball as pain ripped through his abdomen.

Karl took the crusty cloth Adam had earlier set to dry near the wash basin, soaked it, and laid it on his forehead. "You're lucky to die now before Walter comes," he said.

Adam knew better. He and Jess had once helped torch a church that had been used as a makeshift hospital after Typhoid wiped out nearly everyone in the town, and he wished that Walter would have shot him dead at the bar.

He closed his eyes and prayed for death to visit him sooner than later, but death didn't visit him at all. It was Walter who came just before dawn.

"I can't believe I found you after all those years," he sneered. "Finally, I can return the favor."

"Just let me die," Adam breathed.

"You don't get to die."

Walter pushed Adam's head to the side and ran a thumb from his ear to his collar bone. He slid his hand around to the back of his head and jerked him up.

"You get to live forever, like all vampires do."

Adam felt a sharp, stabbing pain and his body stiffened from the shock as Walter bit into his jugular vein. He thrashed and clawed at Walter's back, but the vampire's grip was vicelike. Weakened by the fever, confused and terrified, his vision tunneled, and he found himself hypnotized by the rhythmic squelching sound Walter made each time he swallowed.

Soon, Adam's body relaxed under the larger man's weight, and he was ready to let himself slip away, but the fear of death fired one last burst of adrenaline into his heart. Though his mind would not give up, he knew his body was taking its last breaths. It was then that Walter released him and bit down on his own wrist, letting the blood drip into Adam's mouth.

Walter's blood tasted like black pepper, a spice Adam would despise for the rest of his days; but as he licked it from his lips, it also tasted like life and that adrenaline surge gave him an overwhelming desire for more.

Even so, he turned his head away, rasping, "Why are you doing this?"

Walter said nothing, but he knelt and placed his bleeding wrist near Adam's mouth. He laughed as Adam wrestled with his shame in a losing battle against his will to live. But as he drank the blood, Adam's head cleared and his limbs woke with a new strength, strength he'd never even known as a young man. Walter tried to pull back, but Adam tightened his grip, biting down harder and harder until Walter had to tear himself away, giving up a mouthful of his flesh.

Walter drew back his fist to beat him, but a beam from the sunrise played across his arm with a sizzle. Snarling from the pain, he backed off and ran down the hall, leaving Adam alone on the blood-soaked cot.

Chapter Twelve

Adam raised a hand to the sunlight and discovered with dismay that his skin burned as well, though it healed remarkably fast. He covered the window and locked himself in as the spirits of the miners who had died in the bunkhouse began to show themselves in alarming numbers. They appeared to wish him no harm but even if they had, there was nothing he could do. Exhaustion overtook him and he crawled under the cot, sleeping so hard that he never even heard the day crew blasting his dynamite at the Copper Queen.

He woke that night with a start. Slamming his forehead against the underside of the cot, Adam realized with fresh horror that it had not been a dream. He tossed the cot aside and stared in the mirror, nodding a tense greeting to the spirits hovering behind him.

His clothes were sticky with blood, but the puncture wounds on his neck had mended themselves into small round scars. He stretched his arms overhead, noting that though the aches and pains he'd developed over the years weren't completely gone, they were much abated. In fact, but for a nagging thirst, he felt damn good.

He changed into his only other shirt and took a drawstring pouch from a secret pocket sewn on the inside of his trousers. Having counted out what it would take for a bath and a shave at the brothel, he replaced the pouch and looked in the mirror again. He pushed his top lip over his teeth, but nothing there had changed.

In those few minutes, his nagging thirst had developed into a near ravenous craving. Water was scarce in Bisbee but there would be beer at the brothel, so he hurried outside. In the entryway, he choked on the stench that fanned in from the streets. It had always been bad but that night the waves coming off the garbage and the horse shit mingled with the mine polluted air in a haze that made Adam's eyes water.

On his way up the gulch, his lips dried out and he began to shake from thirst. As he reached to scoop a handful of putrid water from a puddle in the mud, a large boot kicked him away.

"You need blood," Karl said.

"I already had some." The memory sickened him.

"Fresh blood."

"No." Adam put his hands over his face. "I won't do that again."

Karl ushered him under the balcony at the side of the brothel and took a canteen from around his neck. "Drink this."

Adam took a long swig and then doubled over to retch from the foul taste of it. His thirst lingered but after several waves of dry heaves, it had subsided enough that he stopped shaking.

"That was from the slaughterhouse," Karl explained with a shrug.

Adam threw the canteen away and shook Karl by the shoulders, shouting, "What is happening to me?"

"You need blood to live now, but listen to me," he forced Adam to meet his eyes, "you must never drink from another vampire again and never, ever drink from the dead." A touch of encouragement entered his voice then as he warned, "A wooden stake will kill you, but it will kill him too. Remember that."

Karl turned on his heel with no intention of answering any more of Adam's questions in such a public place. "Oh and," he looked over his shoulder with a final bit of advice, "stay out of the sun."

A loud argument came from inside, followed by the screams of women and several gun shots. Karl ducked away and Adam blended in with the crowd that poured into the street to watch. He craned his neck to locate Karl but then thought better of it. They were both in danger, but there was no knowing how Karl would suffer if Walter found out he had helped him.

There was more screaming and then people began to drift away. When the crowd finally dispersed, two men lay dead in the dirt and one of them was Karl. His head was severed from his body, just like Mr. Carson's.

The town he'd called home for three years suddenly felt utterly foreign to him and Adam turned in circles looking for something familiar to cling to. Behind him he heard a shriek and spun around to see a prostitute he knew running through the mud, chased by a miner. She stumbled over some rocks and as she hit the ground, she started pitching them at her attacker.

The miner jerked her up by the shoulders and

taunted, "No charge for your favorite, right?"

In the time it took for the miner to shove her against the wall, Adam was across the street throwing him to the ground. The girl dashed away, and the miner was so dazed by the force of Adam's hit that he lay in the mud drifting in and out of consciousness.

Adam loomed over him, listening to his heartbeat. He licked his lips and cut his tongue on the new fangs that had lowered for the victim. He fell to his knees, praying for God to take the craving away, but too many minutes passed with no change. He grabbed the miner by the collar and thought for a second that he could let him go, but those throbbing veins were too much for a brand-new vampire ignore.

His blood tasted of bitter dandelion root and Adam gagged at first, then gulped it down, feeling nothing short of euphoria as the craving dissipated.

His previously jumbled thoughts crystallized as he set the lifeless miner aside. The man was a would-be rapist sure, but who was Adam to judge?

He was the devil. Walter had made him so and then killed Karl, leaving him to figure out his new life alone. He stared up at the stars but didn't bother to pray again, deciding that if he was the devil, he would do his part and send the bad men to Hell ahead of him. It was the first time that Adam killed for blood and the last time he ever talked to God.

* * *

Laura sprang from her seat and wrapped her arms around him. There was nothing she could say to ease his pain, yet Adam was comforted by her silent act of tenderness; and, by the fact that Bash didn't throw him from the house after hearing his story.

He kissed her cheek and poured himself some more tea. "I couldn't go back to the mine and work in such close quarters with those men, and I didn't dare look for Miss—" he caught himself before mentioning the woman he'd hoped to take to the mountains and, again, his friends didn't ask him about her.

"How in the hell did you get out of there?" Bash wondered.

"That's another long story but believe it or not Jess and Cory found me. We hid out in Naco before coming here."

"To Chuparosa?"

Adam nodded. "We fixed up a short wagon with three heavy tarps. It was cramped with gear and hot as hell–hard, hard travellin' that took us longer than a month. I watched over them at night and every now and then a couple of murderous thieves would show up to meet my, um, needs." He smiled to himself. "I believe Cory would have lost *all* affection for me if it had taken one second longer for her to get home."

"Cory?" Laura was more fascinated by the Jess aspect of Adam's story with each new detail.

"His wife. They lived out their days right here."

"In Chuparosa?" Bash tapped Drew's arm and chuckled, "This has always been a one-horse town."

"I'll be damned," Drew said. He was beginning to think that the Chuparosa connection was more than a coincidence but kept that to himself as the shadow of grief passed over Adam's face. There was no knowing how many loved ones he'd lost to old age over the years, and it would be cruel to press him out of mere curiosity.

Adam stared hard at Bash for a second. "You remind me of him. Of Jess."

"Yeah?"

"Yeah." He rubbed his eyes, a vampire's exhaustion creeping in. "I don't know what Walter's game is this time, but he's out there now—baiting me."

"Baiting us," Bash corrected, "and we'll figure it out together."

Chapter Thirteen

Adam opened his mouth to protest and then remembered Lucifer's warning. He hated that once again the people he loved risked their lives for him, but he would put his trust in them, hoping that Cara stayed out of the fray until it was over, and that they lived to tell her about it.

Laura guided him away from the window as the sunrise began to peek through the blinds. She reached out to slap them shut, making a face as she noticed Chuck pulling in the driveway with Sam Parker.

The passenger door bounced back open after Sam slammed it shut and he made fun of the county vehicle's condition all the way up to the house.

"That piece of shit ain't fit for the road." His complaint echoed in from the porch. "I bet they'd give you a new one if you show 'em the mileage count. It must be some kind of record."

"It runs, man." Chuck held the window in place while using his hip to push Sam's door closed. "Besides, we don't need any extra attention from Phoenix. Not right now."

"I'm pretty sure my seat belt didn't even click."

"Pussy."

Inside, Laura said to Bash, "I wonder what this is about."

His eyes widened as he peered through slats. Though Chuck was still a bit unsteady on his feet, he looked like a completely different man than the one Bash had visited that morning. Sam was giving him a hard time, but he was watching, ready to catch him if he fell.

Ushering them in, Bash pulled Chuck into a bear hug. "You're looking pretty damn good!"

"I guess the poison has run its course." He was going to tell them about an unsettling dream he'd had that afternoon, from which he woke feeling much better but in a peculiar way; then he eyed their bandages and blurted, "What happened to you guys?"

"Demon burns," Drew said with a yawn, pouring himself more coffee.

Bash poured Sam and Chuck cups of their own and started another pot as he relayed an abridged version of the events on the butte. "And I'll tell you what," he poked at his bandages, "they were gangly little fuckers but man they were strong."

"Hey sweetheart." Sam took a sip and smiled at Laura over the rim of his cup.

She glared at him. "Done any more night fishing?"

"Wish you'd been there. We could have used the A-Team on our side."

"Wait, you're saying the Devil did this to you?" Chuck picked up Bash's arm for a closer look.

"No, it was one of his demons."

"Lucifer is an angel, by the way. Not a devil." Drew corrected once again.

Though Sam had been menacing Laura, he heard every word Bash said and very little of it made sense to him. "Why would Lucifer, *the angel*, care about—"

"It was a warning for me," Adam interrupted. "Someone from my past has made an appearance and he's not here to reminisce."

"Well," Sam traded looks with Chuck and said, "that makes our visit timely." He took out his phone and laid it on the kitchen table. "Seth reported more vampire activity in the White Mountains."

"In those caves on the Rim?" Bash's spine began to tingle.

"Nope." He opened an email and cued up a video. "This guy moved into an abandoned hunter's shack outside of Snowflake with nothin' but a huge steamer trunk and a couple of goons."

Sam pressed play on the video of a stocky man overseeing the unloading of a trunk from the bed of a Ford F-150 to a small cabin in the woods. It was dark and a light flurry of snow had begun to fall. In the dim porch light they could make out little more than his shoulder length hair under a leather porkpie hat, his barn coat and his boots.

Seth had been at a distance while he filmed and, though at one point the man faced the camera, they could not clearly see his face. Just before he turned to go inside, he spit tobacco in the snow.

Adam gripped the edge of the table and said, "That's him. That's Walter."

Bash picked up the phone and rewatched the video several times, searing the image of Walter Sallow into his brain. "There's no more of this recording?"

Sam shook his head. "Seth was on his own and he didn't wait around for them to smell him. He set up trail cams on his way out, so we'll get more."

"He thinks they might have a woman workin' with 'em," Chuck added. "A witness says he saw them together before he came across a dead park ranger leaving the Lakeside station a couple of hours earlier. We're waitin' on the station's security camera footage, but Seth didn't see her at the cabin."

Laura's expression turned stony again. "Could it be Cara?" She wondered aloud.

Bash raised an eyebrow at her, surprised that she would suspect her friend with no other evidence in hand.

"Nah," Sam said, "she doesn't fit the description." It was still unclear to him why Lucifer himself would bother with a warning to a vampire so, before they could think more about the woman, he turned to Adam and asked, "Why do you get personalized message service from Hell?"

Adam shrugged and teetered near the table as the need to sleep weighed him down.

Laura took his arm. "You'll stay here today." They had a guest room with only one window that could easily be darkened and she led him down the hall, ignoring his refusals.

Sam took careful notes as Bash and Drew told them the rest of Lucifer's warning.

"Good to know, but I'm not gonna lie, I'm glad I wasn't there," he said with a shiver. "That's a meeting I plan to put off for many more years."

After putting Adam to bed, Laura stood behind the

couch listening to the men talk. Though the furnace had kicked on, she shook as if it were below zero in the house. She too had accepted that her fate included a future meeting with Lucifer, and, like Sam, she had blithely assumed it would be much later.

A theory was forming in her mind regarding Cara's whereabouts, but she hoped that she was wrong. If not, they could all meet the king of Hell's angels before the week was over.

Drew's bandage had started to slip, so she peeled it off, inspected his wound and replaced it.

"Oh," he laughed, though his face twisted with pain, "now I get the good nurse."

She reached up and gave Bash's shoulders a squeeze, saying, "I'm going to take a shower."

What she really wanted was to talk to her sister. As a witch, if she was going to help Adam, there was work to be done. She didn't even get the bedroom door closed behind her before pressing Sarah's number on her phone.

"This Walter," Drew said once she'd left the room, "there's something wrong with him. If he wants to die so bad, why doesn't he just—"

"He's a batshit crazy motherfucker and we're gonna have to put him down," Bash grumbled.

"You know what that means, right man?" Chuck asked him.

Bash hesitated for a second, ran a hand through his hair, then nodded his head.

"If you're sure, buddy," Sam slapped Bash on the back, "we gotta sleep on a plan." He tapped his watch.

Though he was exhausted, Drew protested, "It's seven in the morning."

In a voice tight and low, Bash said, "We're on vampire time now."

Chapter Fourteen

After shooing the others away, Bash stood listening for a moment outside the guest room door. Laura left it slightly ajar so Carl could come and go as he pleased, but after taking a peek inside, it didn't look to Bash like Carl would do much wandering around. Adam was under the quilt, sleeping on his side facing the door and the dog was curled up at the end of the bed. Carl had Adam's legs pinned down with his weight, but it looked like that was a familiar and comfortable position for them both.

Adam had tried to explain to Laura that only direct sunlight could hurt him, but she hung a thick throw blanket over the curtains so that not even a sliver of light could get through. Carl perked his head up, but Bash waved a dismissive hand to indicate that there was nothing to worry about, so he laid down and went back to sleep.

It was then that Bash made the connection between Carl the dog and Karl from the mine, both of whom looked out for Adam regardless of how dangerous it was to do so. There had to be more to the story behind his friendship in Bisbee and Bash made a mental note to find the right time to ask him about it later. If there was a later.

The shower came on as he stepped into the main bedroom and Watson posted himself outside the bathroom door where he would pace until Laura emerged. She had drawn their curtains as well and lit a candle on the dresser. He leaned over it, inhaled, and furrowed his brows. He preferred the lavender and vanilla scented perfume she made for herself but, given their predilection for danger, she would often burn rose around the house to help them relax.

Having double checked the locks on the windows and the revolver in the nightstand, he took a pair of sweatpants from the dresser drawer and as he changed, he grinned at the state of their bed, unmade and in total disarray.

Before Adam visited them earlier, Laura had tackled Bash while he was putting away his laundry. They fell together rolling tangled in the covers, laughing and wriggling until passion overtook their playfulness.

What started as an afternoon of tedious chores had progressed into hungry kisses and cries of pleasure and then overnight devolved into an undertaking that terrified him more than their meeting with Lucifer. Fighting vampires was a job he'd done in the past and one that no candle, no weapon, no spell could ever calm him enough to prepare for.

Lying in bed he tried to tamp down his fears but could not keep out thoughts of the forest and the cave where vampires once hung him upside down with plans of torturing him to death. It was an awful fight, but he survived it without being bitten. Soon afterward there were more battles with even more disturbing creatures, and he was able to convince himself over time that a vampire's bite may not be the worst way to die.

That is, until he was bitten during one of those later battles. He rubbed at the dime-sized scars on his forearm left by Adam's razor-sharp fangs. He'd volunteered his blood to save his friend that night, but he never forgot the anguished look on Adam's face as he tried to balance how much blood it would take to stay alive with how much taken would kill Bash. Truth be told the volumes had been too close for either of them to dwell on after the fact.

That sacrifice renewed in Bash abject terror of not only being murdered by a vampire but, thanks to Adam's story about Walter, of being turned into one himself. For Adam's sake he wanted to understand that life but unlike Adam, he would kill himself before he ever took part in it.

His head ached and his heart thumped, and the room began to close in on him as his panic spiraled, threatening to unravel all that was left of his sense of control. Soon he felt Laura's arms around him as she slid into bed and spooned him from behind. His breathing slowed and he rolled over to pull her close.

"You're not on vampire time," he whispered in her ear.

"I'm on whatever time you are." She put her finger to his lips when he opened his mouth to object. "I know you want to argue about that, but don't."

It was a conversation he would need to have with her, but as she ran her hands through his thick gray hair and snuggled into his bare chest, he decided just to hold her for a while. So many dreadful things had come to light in the last twelve hours that he struggled to get his mind around it all, and for him that was saying something.

He watched the shadows play across the bedroom ceiling for what seemed like hours and when anxiety finally gave way to exhaustion, a movie he knew all too well began to play in his mind.

He dreamed he was far in the desert, scaling a mountain with no trail. It was difficult to breathe, and his shirt was soaked through from the exertion, so he paused on the landing in front of a small cave to wipe the sweat away with his sleeve. Shielding his eyes from the sun with his hand, he squinted around for his cowboy hat, but it wasn't there. In fact, there was no one else there either.

His friends were usually in his dreams, trapped in a loop of danger created by his subconscious to distract him from the messages he was supposed to be receiving. Difficult as it was to ignore their suffering, the Archangel Michael had taught him how to see through those distractions, but this time there were none. Even the air was still, so his guard was up as he peered inside the cave.

He called for Laura and when she didn't answer he called for Drew and then Adam and Chuck. A heavy pang of loneliness hit him so deep in the chest that he sagged against the wall of the cave until a familiar voice broke the silence.

"Did you lose something cowboy?"

Bash jumped and spun around to see Thomas, his wings fully unfurled—a gesture he usually reserved for making a point of some kind—and his hand holding out his hat.

Bash snatched it away from him and put it on. "What's happening here?"

Thomas ignored his question. "Where's Laura?"

When Bash hesitated, Thomas grew stern. "Where is my daughter?"

"I don't know," he snapped. Bash was annoyed by Thomas on a good day, and it had not been one of those. "She's safe as long as she's not here."

A hot wind blew from the inside the cave, twisting his wings and forcing Thomas backward end over end off the ledge.

"Thomas!" Bash dove to catch him but when he scanned the expanse, Thomas was gone. "Shit."

"If she's not with you, *you're* not safe."

It was another familiar voice behind him, but Bash was reluctant to face it. The deafening buzz that accompanied it was unmistakable and his stomach churned as he slowly turned to find Lucifer standing amidst a den of rattlesnakes at the center of the cave.

"Jesus Christ!" Bash leapt away and then froze as two of the rattlers wrapped themselves around his ankles and held him still.

Lucifer appeared to him almost as before, the difference was that his eyes had become narrow with pale slits for irises and as he spoke his tongue flicked out long and forked. He reached around and jerked Laura from the darkness behind him, shoving her to her knees in front of Bash, face to face with the snakes.

Torn away at the sleeve, she still wore the t-shirt she'd put on for bed. "You bastard!" she screamed and rubbed her hands together.

"Baby no!" Bash reached out to stop her from

engulfing Lucifer in the electricity lacing through her fingers. There was no telling what he would do to her in response.

"See what I mean? Don't discount her power, Sebastian," he hissed, "and don't forget about the other woman either."

"You said you were going to find out her plans," Bash snapped. He was close to hyperventilating, looking frantically from Laura's fury to Lucifer's sickly augmented facade to the snakes at his feet. His stomach turned as dozens of little ones slithered out of the angel's cardigan pockets and made soft thuds as they hit the dirt.

"Focus!" Lucifer snapped his fingers making the loudest clap of thunder Bash had ever heard.

Somewhere in the back of his mind, Michael reminded Bash to discard the distractions. He closed his eyes and though it took some mental gymnastics, he drew his attention from the snakes and searched the dream for the message.

"Cara," he breathed, "and..." Flickering in the corner of his mind was the blurry image of a woman with purple hair. One of the rattlesnakes unwound itself from his ankle and slithered up his jeans along the inside of his thigh. It was thick and heavy and soon it was making its way up his chest.

"Let the women handle the women," Lucifer ordered.

Bash held his breath and squeezed his eyes to keep them shut, trying to control his breathing as the snake inched around his neck. When he felt the flick of its tongue on his chin, he could no longer stifle his screams. Though he knew the danger, he reached up to pull it away but grasped only at his skin. The snake was gone.

The one on his ankle had disappeared as well and when he looked out, the only thing left of Lucifer and Laura were the depressions in the dirt where they'd been. Loneliness engulfed him again and he put his hands over his ears as if he could somehow block it out. Then he fell to his knees, giving in to the stress and letting out a tormented roar.

Shivering but sweating, he twitched awake and as his eyes adjusted from the bright sunlight of his dream to the darkness of the bedroom, he reached for Laura. She was as far away from him in the bed as she could be, close to falling over the edge and thrashing about in her sleep.

"Laura," he pulled her close. "Baby, wake up."

She shrieked and backed into the headboard, staring as if she didn't know him.

"It's me, baby, it's me." He held his hands out to her and when she finally recognized him, she buried herself in his arms.

He noticed that her t-shirt was torn at the sleeve and a dreadful thought occurred to him. When he pulled back the covers, her knees were skinned up and streaked with dirt.

Through gritted teeth he asked, "Were you in the desert with me just now?"

"And the snakes," she sniffed with irritation.

"God dammit."

It was too much to process so they just held each other, saying nothing else about it for the time being.

Bash had a compass tattoo over the upper right quadrant of his chest and over time Laura had figured out that she could get him to settle down by lightly tracing her fingers along its points. Soon his grip on her relaxed and his breathing evened out into a low snore. She guided him from his back to his side and he quieted completely.

She, however, was too furious to sleep. Bash had figured out that she was physically in his nightmare, but she would have to find the right time later to fill him in on what he hadn't seen. How Lucifer had kicked at the foot of their bed to wake her before dragging her screaming into the desert.

For proof she would offer the scorches in the area rug from where she'd tried to fight him off with her power. Though he easily deflected the hastily gathered fireballs she threw at him, he was enraged by her resistance.

"You will not be the reason for my failure, witch," he'd snarled at her before covering them both in those damn snakes.

She shuddered, remembering the feel of their smooth bellies slithering around her limbs while the two of them traveled through the dream. How he had charmed the men in her life she would never know. Andrew believed him possibly the most misunderstood creature ever and Adam thought of *himself* as more of a devil than Lucifer.

She didn't trust his motivation for a minute and knew in her bones that he was going to wreak havoc in their lives. That meant she would have to up her magical game to his level in order to compete. Or—and she was afraid this was more likely—lower it to his level.

Chapter Fifteen

Just after sunset, Bash put on a t-shirt, stumbled out of the bedroom with a yawn and flipped open the blinds to the darkening sky.

He ran a hand through his hair, mumbling, "Jesus, here we go."

Laura handed him a cup of coffee and he brought it up to inhale the aroma.

"Thanks baby."

"I hope you're hungry." She placed a plate piled with pancakes in the middle of the table. "We might as well flip flop everything and start with breakfast for dinner, or I guess it's just breakfast for breakfast...or whatever."

Bash chuckled and slapped Adam on the back. "I'm more concerned about whether or not he's hungry."

Adam was at the stove moving bacon from a cast iron skillet to some paper towels and he knew Bash was only half joking. It was accepted that Adam would never hurt them, but blood was a biological need of his that could become quite a bit more than an inconvenience in the coming days.

"I intend to go hard on those pancakes." He took a seat next to Bash at the table and looked him in the eyes. "But I won't need anything *else* for a couple of weeks."

"Got it."

Bash understood but, to Adam's dismay, he remained tense. They ate in silence, the three of them lost in their own thoughts, until Laura's cell phone rang.

"Hi Chuck...yeah, he left his phone on the charger in the bedroom...okay, here he is."

Adam and Laura cleared the table while Bash paced the house on the phone. Once the dishwasher was humming along, Adam kissed her on the cheek and put his hand on the doorknob to leave.

"Thanks for everything, beautiful. Have him call me when—"

"Hang on, Adam." Bash waved a hand to stop him from leaving. "Alright Chuck, we'll see you in a few hours." He ended the call and started for the bedroom.

"Chuck's gonna stay here in town to hold down the fort, but he says we can use his cabin in Pinetop as a base of operations. We'll get your things and then Sam will meet us at the station in a few hours to convoy with us up north. Does that work for you?"

Though Adam would have given anything not to have them involved in his predicament at all, he nodded.

"Give me ten minutes."

Bash reappeared dressed in jeans, hiking boots and a long sleeve Henley with a flannel shirt over it. Adam noted with amusement that unless he owned several in the same color, it was the flannel Laura wore the night before. His revolver was holstered on his hip, and he carried a large duffel bag over his shoulder which he dropped on the floor before rummaging through the pantry.

"Baby, where're those...oh, wait...never mind." He gathered up a white plastic grocery bag full of aluminum cans and said, "We'll be back in a little bit to pick you up."

As Laura pulled an ice chest and another enormous first aid kit from the hall closet, she said, "I'll be ready," kissed Bash and pressed the first number on her speed dial as soon as the door was closed after them.

* * *

The tension in the cab of the truck was palpable on the ride to Adam's house. Bash was frustrated, angry and afraid, and Adam mistook those emotions to be directed at him.

"Listen Bash," he started, "after what my kind did to you, you must hate—"

Bash shook his head. "They were not *your* kind," he argued, "and you know I don't hate vampires." He gave him a wry look. "I hate murderous fucking monsters."

A lump formed in Adam's throat. That Bash had lived through enough to draw a distinction between him and a murderous fucking monster was as touching as it was alarming.

"Still, you don't owe me," he said, "I'll understand if..." His voice trailed off as Bash took an unexpected turn down a dark stretch of unmarked dirt road. He drove until they came to a dead end at the base of a mountain and turned off the ignition.

"We don't owe each other anything." Bash gripped the steering wheel, keeping his eyes forward and his jaw set. "That's the point."

Adam hung his head. "I guess I'm still getting used to the idea. It's been a long time since I've had a friend like you."

They were only a few miles from the paved road, but the desert seemed particularly dark outside the glow of the headlights. Black and twisted Palo Verde branches appeared to reach for the hood of the truck, and stretching out from the passenger side was a desolate clearing that had been created by lightening fires from a summer monsoon storm.

"So...what are we doing out here?" Adam wondered.

"Shooting." Bash flipped the headlights to a dimmer setting and reached into the backseat for the bag of cans.

"Shooting?"

They hadn't been able to find the time in weeks, but the two of them frequently went night shooting at the Ben Avery range. They'd bonded over a shared love of the old west–Adam had lived it and Bash had wanted to–and those nights at the range gave them the opportunity to talk about it. Their conversations of late often strayed from history and though the friendship they'd developed was priceless to Adam, he'd never allowed himself to acknowledge how much it meant to Bash until then.

Even so, Bash needed to know for sure that the two of them were on exactly the same page before they went up north to fight an evil that only Adam truly understood. Their mutual trust could be the one thing that kept them alive if things went sideways and, since they always did, Adam agreed that taking the extra time to shore it up before they left was the right move.

Ben Avery was too far from Chuparosa for a quick shoot, so Bash made do with what Adam felt was even better. The clearing was once home to several Velvet Mesquite trees that had been reduced to nothing more than a wide, misshapen circle of burned-out stumps to place cans atop. From the middle of the circle, they had a little more than fifty feet between themselves and their targets on either side.

"I know you've got it with you," Bash said when they finished setting up.

Indeed, Adam always had his pistol with him, concealed in a small holster inside the waistband of his jeans. No matter how many different professions he had worked since gunfighting for pay, he would never go anywhere without it. He tucked the tail of his shirt behind the grip, but Bash's hand was already hovering over his own holster, so Adam backed out of the circle to gather their extra ammo from the glove compartment. Since they practiced together so often, Bash always had a box for Adam's nine-millimeter.

Bash drew his pistol, shot three cans in front of him, then spun and shot the three behind him. They reset the targets and took turns at quick draw, blowing the cans off the stumps until they were little more than sharp shreds of aluminum.

Adam felt that Bash could have made a name for himself as a shootist back in the day, but he would not have wished that life on anyone. Besides, given Adam's typical client back then they might have found themselves at odds on occasion and he preferred that they enjoy a genuine friendship rather than tenuous professional courtesy.

By the time their targets were spent, the men were full of adrenaline and dopamine, laughing and taunting each other as they gathered up what was left of the cans. The exercise had broken the tension between them and though it didn't do much to alleviate his deep-seated fear of what was to come, it was a much-needed stress reliever for Bash.

Chapter Sixteen

"Grab a beer, I won't be long."

While Adam packed, Bash wandered his house, taking mental notes on various items that caught his interest. He was a man who could appreciate things that were made to last and throughout the house there were several simple but solid antique pieces that Bash wondered if Adam had built himself.

He'd only been there a few times and only with Laura at dinner parties that were alive with food and wine and the polite conversation of couples. Polite as it could be given the mixed company of witches, vampires, preachers, and lawmen who regularly fought angels and demons and goblins, but that was their life.

In the kitchen he took two beers from the refrigerator and popped the tops, laughing to himself at their fancy new trash can. You needed only to wave your hand over the sensor to open it and he was certain it must have been a Cara purchase. Her willful, confident energy lingered throughout the house, and if Bash could so acutely feel her absence, he thought

Adam must be dying inside. When he tossed the caps, he stooped to pick up a crumpled piece of paper from the floor.

He waved his hand over the trash can again to throw it out but the detective in him could not ignore Cara's handwriting on the page.

"Damn her." He'd tried not to pass judgment since hearing that she left, but after reading the note, Bash's heart ached for his friend.

"She has a way with words, doesn't she?" Adam picked up his beer and downed half of it.

"Don't lose this." Bash smoothed out the paper, folded it up and handed it to him. "It's her promise."

"We'll see." Adam gave him a thin smile and put it in his breast pocket.

"It's not easy but we have to let strong women be strong." Bash took a swig of his beer and leaned against the counter. "I fucked that up with Laura in the beginning."

"All women are strong, Bash, they have no choice. You and me? We feed off that strength, it's unlike ours in every way and we depend on it. That must be why we feel so compelled to protect them."

Bash sniffed. "And here I thought I was in love."

"That, my friend," Adam said, "adds a whole different layer of complication."

"Well," Bash conceded, "you've got more experience than I'll ever have."

"Experience sure," Adam shrugged, "but I could never put it to good use. In all these years, I've truly loved only two women, and both have cost me a huge chunk of my soul." He finished his beer. "No matter what happens between her and I, Cara will be the last."

He unzipped a pocket on the side of his duffel, then reached into a cabinet under the sink. He felt around and pulled out a wooden cylinder roughly the size of a dinner fork. He uncorked the top and motioned for Bash to open a blue velvet pouch that fell onto the table.

"That might come in handy."

The pouch contained a hatpin made of solid silver, topped with a turquoise bead resting in a filigree cup.

"Silver," Bash said, running his fingers over the pin.

"I had that made special, *before* I was turned," Adam explained.

Bash's eyes widened with realization, and he put the hat pin back in the pouch. "You can't touch it now, can you?"

Adam shook his head, but his expression softened as he zipped it into the pocket. "Hell, you want to talk about experience? The woman I made that for tried to get me killed more than once."

Bash threw his head back and laughed at the way Adam grinned when he spoke, as if those brushes with death were some of his fondest memories.

Prescott, Arizona 1878

Passersby looked on in surprise as the four dusty men on horseback rode out from the pines. No one expected them to come back at all, let alone with Royal Tucker in tow. The horsemen paused in front of the courthouse which doubled as a saloon.

"Well, that's handy," Jess said, mulling over his plans for later.

"Towns got all the amenities, John," Adam added, "but where's the jail?" He was anxious to be rid of their prisoner and even more anxious to be rid of the badge on his chest.

"Got no jail." The territorial sheriff who rode with them disclosed the information with a defensive grunt and urged his horse alongside Tucker's. "But he ain't goin' nowhere this time."

Jess arched an eyebrow at Adam. "No jail?"

A large brown quarter horse in the middle of their party carried the battered Royal Tucker. A rope around his chest bound his arms to his sides and the rope at the end of a noose around his neck was tied to Adam's saddle horn. They'd settled upon that unseemly arrangement after a number of false starts out of Jerome. That and the shotgun Jess kept aimed at Royal's kidneys for the last thirty miles had taken much of the fight out of their prisoner. Still, they couldn't blame him for trying. He was going to hang the next day, and everyone but him would be glad to see it done.

Two months earlier while Adam and Jess drove the stagecoach from Jerome to Prescott, they came across the previous stage, shot up, overturned and gutted. The driver was dead, the miners' payroll was gone, and the only passenger was a woman who'd been pistol whipped and left for dead on the side of the road.

They raced her to Prescott and when she was strong enough, she testified that Royal Tucker, a known felon from the area, had committed the crime. Of that they had no doubt but while she was unconscious, Jess had searched her things for some clue to her identity. He found a note that had Royal's name, the name of a different Tucker family member, and an address in Topeka, Kansas written in feminine script.

"You need to keep an eye on Miss Betty Brown,"

Jess had warned the Sheriff.

Women were so scarce in town though that John didn't dare look very hard into a connection between Betty and Royal. Even if they did believe she was involved, no one would believe that the diminutive, blonde wasn't just another victim of his, so he burned the note in the fireplace and sent them back on the stagecoach route.

Royal was captured by a posse and found guilty at trial, but he escaped before he could hang for his crimes. It was an unfortunate addition to the Sheriff's recent public relations woes and the town was outraged by his incompetence. John had trouble forming another posse and Royal made it all the way to Jerome before he and his reluctant new deputies, Carson and Colter, caught up with him.

Now they followed the Sheriff to a log cabin next to a boarded-up shanty storefront. Both were once owned by an assayer who died of ague five months after he arrived, and the town had commandeered the properties until a new assayer could be found.

Typically, since there was no jail, the army would provide round the clock guard service while prisoners awaited trial or, in this case, execution. But the beleaguered Sheriff was reluctant to spend more tax money on that service, especially since Royal Tucker had outsmarted his army guards once already. The rate for a deputy sheriff's time was considerably lower and the town had more confidence in Adam and Jess anyway.

"No fucking way," Adam said, staring at the shanty in disbelief.

"Suckers," Royal snorted.

"It's only for tonight," John pleaded. "I'll hang his sorry ass in the morning."

"Fine." Jess gave Royal a shove and he hit the ground with an 'oof' and a thud.

"Bet that hurt some," Adam jeered.

They hammered pegs in the wall of the shack and secured him to a corner with just enough slack to use the chamber pot and then settled in with their shotguns to play a mind game they called, *which body parts will we blow off if Tucker makes a move?*

An hour or so later, there was a knock at what was passing for a door. A wide gap between it and the jamb, for which their complaints had fallen on deaf ears, allowed the cold night air to whip through the shanty but made it easy for Jess to nudge it open using the barrel of his shotgun.

He quickly lowered the weapon when he glimpsed a young woman wearing a dingy linen apron and carrying a large tray. Her thick, strawberry blonde hair was gathered in a long braid down her back and tiny freckles dotted most of her skin.

"This ain't no place for you, honey."

Keeping her head down, she pushed her way past him and said, "The sheriff told me to bring you some food."

It had been at least twenty-four hours since they'd eaten and their stomachs growled as she uncovered the tray, revealing three metal plates piled with some kind of fried meat and smothered in white gravy. They'd even been given two biscuits each.

"Our shy little savior," Adam gushed. He gave Royal a plate and didn't bother sitting down at the rickety table before digging into his own.

"What do I call you?" Jess asked the girl.

"Call her a dumb bitch for pouring too much gravy!" Royal bellowed.

Adam backhanded him and snarled, "Shut the fuck up or the only thing you'll be able to chew is gravy."

When they turned their attention back to her, their savior was gone. Though Jess's mood was much improved by the knowledge of her existence, he made sure that Royal Tucker wished for the dawn as much as they did.

Another knock at the door came just before sunup eliciting a wink from Adam.

"You think it's breakfast?"

Jess jumped up and leaned into the gap, grinning. "Are you gonna tell me your name?"

"Jess Carson, you know my name."

His face fell and he flung open the door. "What do you want?"

Betty Brown peeked over the threshold and gave him a smirk. "Good morning to you too, sir." She held out a basket that smelled of bacon and more biscuits. "That mousy girl was on her way over so I—"

"You stole her basket?"

Betty kept her voice soft so as not to wake Tucker, which both Adam and Jess found interesting.

"I wanted to do my part for the local heroes," she gave them a slight curtsy, "so I offered her my assistance."

Adam took the basket and tossed a biscuit at the snoring Royal. "No gravy. That'll please him." Then he added, "And you wanted to make sure we hadn't let him escape overnight."

"It was a reasonable concern."

"Well, as you can see, you don't have to worry," Jess said, ushering her away. "So, go on now."

"Alrighty." She waved over her shoulder. "See you at the picnic."

"It's an execution, Betty," Jess called after her.

He watched Adam watch her sashay down the walk and sighed, "You're gonna go for it, aren't you?"

"She's a troubled little thing, I'll give you that. But what's the worst that could happen?"

Jess ran a hand over his beard and groaned, but before he could recite the dozen or so probable tragedies that came to mind, the sheriff pounded on the door, hollering, "Bring that piece of garbage out here!" Several burly men were with him, ready to drag Royal Tucker to the gallows.

"You two go over to the hotel and get cleaned up," John ordered. "The town wants to give you an award."

Adam shook his head. "How about you pay us instead?"

"Fine." John gave the air a sniff and waved his hand in front of his face. "Still, a chance encounter with a bar of soap wouldn't hurt either of you."

Chapter Seventeen

While Adam checked them into the hotel and arranged for baths, Jess wandered over to a waist high glass case that caught his attention. The sign read 'Bakery', and he'd never seen anything like it. Soon Adam joined him, and they stood ogling a large collection of pastries lined up on the shelves.

"Got a little bit of everything today, boys," the baker said. He was expecting a big crowd for the hanging and had spent the entire night filling up the display.

"What are those little cakes, there?" Jess asked him.

"Those are called cookies. That's real sugar on top."

"I'll be damned."

"Is that peach pie?" Adam touched the glass, smearing it with his finger. "Oh," he wiped at the smear with his handkerchief, making it considerably worse, "sorry about that."

The baker waved off his concern and walked around the case with a clean cloth. "You're the fellas that brought in Tucker, aren't you?" he asked.

"Right now, they're the fellas getting a bath."

As the cheerful, elderly man from registration led them out back, Adam elbowed Jess. The shy girl with the long braid was taking over for him at the desk.

Shaven and scrubbed clean, they felt almost naked as they made their way through the crowd. As Royal Tucker's only surviving victim, Betty had secured a seat of honor near the gallows and waved them over to sit on either side of her. Her calico dress set off the blue in her eyes, set off an ache in Adam's body and set off alarm bells in Jess.

"Look at you all shiny," She cooed at the younger man. "I'll bet that mousy girl threw herself at you this morning."

Jess ignored her and narrowed his eyes at Adam.

"No?" She pressed, "oh well, there's no accounting for taste." She turned her attention to Adam and frowned. "Where's your lunch?"

Having not considered the hanging to be akin to a saloon show, they had earlier purchased tortillas smeared with beans from the back of a wagon and then polished off a couple of apples they'd picked form a tree in the center of town.

Betty shrugged and removed a bulky handkerchief from a drawstring pouch tied around her wrist. From it, she unwrapped a biscuit slathered with butter and orange marmalade that looked just like the kind sold by the bakery man, though they had seen him wrap them in brown paper tied with fancy ribbon for paying customers.

At last, the judge and the sheriff made their way to

the platform and, to a chorus of boos from the crowd, read off the list of crimes Royal Tucker would hang for.

Royal caught sight of Betty and roared as they wrestled him up the steps. Once the hood was over his head, the fight went out of him, and he began to bawl.

The sheriff continued his speech with a plug for the importance of paying taxes, and a new chorus of boos erupted that was directed at him.

Adam took the opportunity to speak into Betty's ear, asking, "How long were you working with him?"

"Working with who?"

"Royal Tucker."

She straightened her back and took a bite of her biscuit, chewing slowly then dabbing delicately at the corner of her mouth with the handkerchief. Her eyes moistened ever so slightly, and she dabbed at them as well.

"I was only trying to get back home to Kansas, but he double crossed me." Jess had leaned in to hear, but she pushed him away. "He was to take the money and that's it. No one was supposed to get hurt, least of all me." For effect, she gingerly touched the scar Royal left on her temple.

"...to hang from the neck until dead." They heard the judge say over the crowd and then they jumped in their seats as the platform dropped from underneath Royal's feet.

The owner of the hardware store approached them to say that the murdered stagecoach driver had been a friend of his. "You done a good thing here," he said, thumbing over his shoulder to where Tucker twitched at the end of his rope. "And you're a very lucky lady," he added, taking Betty's hand in his.

As they chatted Jess pulled Betty aside. "Lucky lady," he repeated, discretely grabbing her wrist. He'd spotted the grip of a little gun nestled between her breasts, and felt the time was right to make himself plain.

"If anything happens to Adam," he hooked a finger in the stays of her corset and gave them a sharp tug, unseating the gun so that it slid down her rib cage. "I'm not above hurting a woman."

Jess had filled out and grown even taller over the years. He was quite proud of his thick beard but remained self-conscious about the disability Walter had given him. With his crippled arm and sad brown eyes, he had once reminded Betty of a stray dog who followed Adam around for scraps.

What she failed to recognize was that the two of them were in fact a devoted brotherhood. She became aware just then that his eyes were soulful, not sad, and the dangerous soul they harbored could see through anyone's mask. She doubted it would be worth the trouble to divide and conquer the two men, but it sure would be fun to see if she could do it.

She lifted her chin and jerked away from him. "I won't bother asking you to trust me," she snapped, adjusting her bodice, "but it is not in my best interest at this time for anything to *happen* to Adam."

"You're sure you don't want the job permanently?" Sheriff John asked as Adam and Jess dropped their badges in his hand. "Either one of you has a good shot at taking over for me in the next election."

It wasn't any more dangerous than anything else

they'd ever done so if not for the miserable income Jess might have considered it. Instead, he stood in solidarity with Adam who said, "Nope."

They were back in the hotel lobby waiting for John to finish counting out their pay, which to Adam's annoyance, he did far too quickly.

"Does that stack look a little short to you?" he muttered to Jess.

"Look here, Adam," John held up his hands in exasperation, "there would be more, but yesterday someone else robbed the god damned stage!"

"Tell you what," Jess offered, eyeing the bakery case, "throw in a slice of peach pie and one of those sugar topped cookies—no two cookies," he flashed a smile for the girl at the desk, "and we'll call it good."

John gave the baker a pleading look and said, "I'm good for it."

"You are not." The baker crossed his arms over his chest. "But if it's for them, it's on me."

"Then everyone is square and I'm out of here." John left the hotel confirming to himself that he would not be running for another term as sheriff.

"No wonder you two are poor as dirt." Betty came up from behind and swiped Adam's room key from his hand.

They weren't poor as dirt per se, but Jess felt it would be wiser not to correct her. At the top of the stairs Adam said, "Hang on to this for me," and handed Jess his money. Betty had let herself into the room, so Jess took that as his cue to move along.

Adam stopped him as he turned away. "You got plans for tonight?"

"There's a couple of prospectors who will pay me

to read their papers for them, and since your aversion to the law has rendered us otherwise unemployed, I'm gonna see about finding us some kind of steady work. *Then* I'm gonna see about that cold beer everyone's talking about downstairs." He grinned from ear to ear. "Maybe that mousy girl will bring me some."

Adam tipped his hat. "Good luck in your endeavors."

Jess gestured vaguely into the room behind Adam, "That one's trouble. Be careful."

"They're all trouble my friend." Adam smirked and closed the door behind him.

The mousy girl, whose name turned out to be Anne Marie, slept in Jess's arms until just after midnight when a shot from next door came through the wall and shattered the picture over his bed.

"God dammit!" Jess ordered Anne Marie to stay low, pulled on his pants and grabbed his gun before sprinting barefoot down the hall. Terrified of what he might find on the other side, he paused to take a deep breath in front of Adam's door before kicking it in.

He found Adam standing alone in his long johns, facing the open window with his hands on his hips.

"Christ almighty!" Jess scanned the tumbled room. "Are you okay?"

He had been led to believe they had a mutually pleasurable evening, but Adam woke to find Betty on the floor digging through his pants pockets. After riding him like he was the last man on earth, she'd told him all about Topeka and had him almost convinced that he could be something special to her someday.

Disappointing as it was to see her trying to rob him, he wasn't all that surprised, and he was glad he'd thought to give Jess his money. He'd watched with grim amusement while she grew more and more frustrated by his empty pockets and then heaved a loud sigh to get her attention.

She jumped up and threw his pants at him. "Are you laughing at me?"

If he were laughing at all it was at their predicament, but his tone was bitter when he said, "I thought you and I had formed an attachment, but I would have paid you for it."

At that Betty had flown into a rage, tipping over the dresser, hurling the lamp, and finally swiping his gun from the belt hanging on the bedpost. "If that's what you think of me Adam Colter then you are a piece of shit."

"Fair enough," he'd agreed as he dodged the furniture, "but you should have asked if you needed money."

When he sprang to take away the gun, she fired a shot above his head, and he recalled with a grimace that she had only just missed him.

"She took one of my guns before she went out the window, but I'm fine." He tried to assure Jess.

Jess was not assured. Still, he left the room hoping his friend had regained some sense. Anne Marie stood in the hall clutching at her chemise looking horrified and when Jess reached out to comfort her, she ran away.

"Shit," he grumbled and shuffled back to his room.

* * *

Bash was so riveted by Adam's story that he never finished his beer. "Jess got the girl but didn't get to keep her," he mused.

"I'm afraid that was something of a running theme of his in those days, poor guy." Adam chuckled. "Even so, Jess had Betty figured for a psycho from the beginning, but I wasn't thinking. Not with my brain anyway."

Bash nodded in sympathy.

"He was right, and she was no good," Adam continued with a sad smile. "Whenever I was doing well, she would turn up all sparkly and sweet trying to ruin my life. It was like God was using her to keep me humble or something. She even showed up in Bisbee right before Walter. In that regard, I suppose he did me a favor because I never saw her again after I was turned."

"You didn't go looking for her? Ever?"

"Sebastian, the last thing the world needed was for *that* woman to learn about vampires."

Chapter Eighteen

Had Seth waited around up north, he would have seen Betty hop down from the red Ford truck as well as several male vampires who piled out of a black Jeep that pulled up beside her. They milled around ignoring each other until Walter whistled for them and then they tromped up the steps of the shack.

"Aren't you assholes going to give me a hand out here?" Betty hollered as she tugged her hastily packed suitcase off the tailgate and let it fall in the snow. As a vampire, she could have lifted the pickup itself if she wanted to, but their lack of respect irritated her. When no response came from the shack, she hoisted the ice chest on one shoulder, the suitcase on the other and stomped inside.

The rest of the gear could get buried in the snow for all she cared. Most of it was stolen anyway. The suitcase had belonged to the woman whose home they'd invaded in Phoenix, but since her travelling days were over, Betty took it along with her coat, her boots, and several pairs of thick hiking socks. She hated the cold and it was lucky that her latest victims were outdoorsy.

The snow wasn't falling that hard, but the wind felt like icy little daggers whipping across her face. She kicked her heels against the wooden steps to dislodge the mud and wet flakes before they soaked her clothes.

"Brrr!" She glared at the dark fireplace and then at Walter. "Are they good for nothing?"

"Get some wood and make a fire," Walter ordered his men.

No one moved until he banged his fist against the wall and then the shortest one took an axe that rested against the empty wood box and slammed the door behind him in a huff.

"Make some food," Walter snapped at Betty.

She opened her mouth to protest but he lowered his fangs with a growl. She stood still for another minute looking from him to the blizzard outside and then thought better of picking a fight. Stepping through the maze of lounging men and gear scattered throughout the cramped space, she made her way to what only just passed for a kitchen in her eyes.

"We had better facilities in the mining camps," she complained, searching the oven for a pilot light.

A two-burner stove sat atop the oven and to the left of it was an unfinished pine two by four fastened to the wall over a grimy stainless-steel utility sink. The long shelf was empty but for a box of salt, a blue enamel coffee percolator, a container of scouring powder and a dry crusted sponge.

She flipped open the coffee pot and gagged. "I doubt this has ever been cleaned."

"You forget where you came from," Walter jeered.

She stared at him in disbelief, thinking it truly

amazing how they could have spent over a hundred years together, yet he only knew the most basic things about her.

She'd never forgotten where she came from. Those memories were at the core of what drove her every decision and every painful, degrading sacrifice that came with them, and she would never go back.

She had to give it to him though. He knew enough to understand that had she been aware Adam was a vampire, her life choices would have been wildly different. He'd only recently chosen to share that pertinent detail with her which was further proof that Walter Sallow was the cruelest man to ever walk the earth.

As if reading her mind, he gave her a knowing, tobacco-stained smile and said, "We could have waited 'til spring to go to Chuparosa but you were in such an all-fire hurry to—"

"Storm's getting stronger." The short vampire blustered into the shack and dropped a pile of wood into the box.

As he busied himself making a fire, the steamer trunk in the middle of the room began to rattle. Walter laughed and gave it a kick, and as a relentless pounding started up from the inside, he dug a set of keys from his pocket and tossed them to one of the other men.

"Easy now," the man said. When he turned the key in the padlock the lid flew open knocking him backward. Before he could push himself up, Cara sprang onto his chest and dragged her fingernails from his eyelids to his chin.

He sank his fingertips into her forearms until she let go and then threw her off of him. She landed hard on the brick hearth and reached out for a burning log, swinging it wide in front of her to keep them back while she stumbled toward the door. She would have ripped it off its hinges to get out, but her strength was all but gone and Walter was across the room before she could even turn the knob. She felt his arm around her neck and once again lost consciousness as he pulled her to his chest in a choke hold.

Cara woke to the searing pain of rusty chains boring into her wrists and ankles. The floor was cold, and she had been dumped unceremoniously in a heap near the center of the room. The energy it took to heal from the gun shots and the lack of fresh blood since had weakened her and her captors knew this, but they weren't taking any chances.

Her vision was blurry, but she could make out the long-haired man from the warehouse, Betty, and at least six other men crowded onto every available seating space. Whatever they were up to, the tiny shack was a poor choice for it. From what she could tell, there was only one bedroom and not enough space in the living room for the rest of them to stretch out. Two wooden walking sticks, a fishing pole and a tackle box indicated that the place hadn't been completely abandoned, but it didn't look like Betty and her friends had killed anyone to take it over.

They balanced bowls of food on their laps, and the absence of any hint of fresh blood in the air told her they were all vampires. What she did smell, in addition to their body odor and the mold in the walls was some kind of chicken soup. Though her stomach growled for it, her insides were on fire with a much deeper hunger.

The vampire she'd scratched was already healing but she'd left deep scars on his face and a grudge in his heart. He noticed as she tried to sit up and put his bowl aside so he could slap her back down. Her face burned as her newly cracked cheek bone bruised, but she remained conscious, stubbornly gazing up at him.

He reared his leg back and she braced herself for a kick in the ribs but like lightening, Betty was on him. She used her entire body to knock him off balance and send him teetering on one foot over the back of the tiny love seat, slopping two hot bowls of soup all over his co-workers.

"Crazy bitch!" He howled, but as he charged for her, Betty ran him through the chest with one of the walking sticks.

Shrieking in pain, he grabbed at the stick to pull it free, but Betty took a log from the fire and lit his clothes.

"Walt, look what she did to me! Walt!" He spun in a few frenetic circles and then stumbled outside, collapsing on the porch. They watched the blaze for a bit and then Walter snapped his fingers, so Betty kicked the dead body into the wet snow and then turned on the others.

"Does anyone else want to try anything stupid?"

They looked to Walter for guidance, but his head had been bent over his bowl of soup the entire time, and he said nothing, so they returned their attention to their own dinners.

Cara could not imagine what Betty's end game was and she doubted they would be granted the privacy for a heart-to-heart talk. For the time being she was simply grateful for an incidence of women helping women and left it at that.

Pale and wild eyed, she pushed herself up again. "Is all of this really necessary?" Holding up her chains, she slurred, "What do you want with me?"

Walter finally spoke up, "Your zip code."

Chapter Nineteen

"My what?"

"Do you know how few vampires there are, blondie?"

Cara shook her head and let it rest against the wall, wincing form the pain of the motion. "This room is one hundred percent vampire," she rasped.

Ignoring her statistics report, he took a bag of tobacco from his vest pocket and stuffed a pinch of it in his cheek.

"I used to think there was no real place for us in this world," he said, "that scratching by in the dark was the only way to exist until the end of time—a miserable life not worth living. Then I stumbled on Chuparosa."

Some of the tobacco had already made its way in between his teeth and she curled her lip in revulsion.

"It seems like a tolerant little town," he said, "with direct access to the Other Side no less. I should not have been surprised to learn that Adam Colter had set himself up there." Walter shook his head and laughed to himself. "Then again, he was always pretending to be a regular man."

Adam? What did he know of Adam? The room suddenly tilted as her mind reeled with realization.

"Wait. Walt? Walter...Walter Sallow. Adam's maker," she whispered.

No wonder Adam had been acting so strangely. The thought of those vampires in Chuparosa filled her with dread, but not as much as learning that she was being used as bait for their trap.

Walter gave Cara a nod of approval and said, "Blondie is a smart woman."

Betty glared at him and waved her hand over Cara's chained, broken body. "Not smart enough," she sniffed, "but then who is?"

It irritated her that Walter had taken to calling Cara 'blondie'. It had always been his name for her and that is why she started dying her hair as soon as the technology became available. She hated Walter, but also that he could replace her so easily.

She was able to walk freely around the room, but Betty knew that she was just as much Walter's prisoner as Cara, and it incensed her. Were it not for the taxes and the tourists he would have been perfectly happy to live until the end of days in that piece of shit shack.

Walter found the progress that came with the passing of time contemptible. He refused to accept any form of technology, making others drive and shop for him while he managed only the most basic tasks of survival. After all those years he could still barely read.

He was a willfully stupid man but even on the few occasions when she'd gotten away for a while, she'd never been able to escape him. The bitch of it all was that it had been her choice. Of course, that didn't mean she hated Cara any less for living the life that could have been hers.

"I left Adam," Cara breathed, "he won't come looking for me."

Betty would never believe that. "You didn't leave him."

"I left him so I could be free to find you...and kill you."

"Excellent work," Betty mocked her, twirling around and striking a 'very much alive' pose, "and here's the real kicker: he would have helped you do it if he'd known you were after me."

He knows both of them. Cara's catastrophic failure was getting worse by the second and she was losing her ability to form rational thoughts. She needed a plan, but first she needed to heal and for that she needed blood, which could possibly show up on the doorstep, but it wasn't likely to do so during a snowstorm. She also needed information and if she could keep her wits about her, Walter seemed in the mood to spill his guts.

"What makes you think you'll be welcome in Chuparosa?" she asked him.

"You," he said.

He waved a coffee cup in Betty's direction and added, "Even if you did leave him, Adam will come here to bargain for your life, and we will negotiate for the town. I did my research and..."

Betty slammed the coffee pot on the sink. "Who did the research?"

He ignored her and said to Cara, "and nobody gives a damn about Chuparosa."

"You might be surprised." Her eyes fluttered closed as she spoke, and she let out a breathy laugh. "If they wouldn't give it up to a fallen angel with the power of Hell on his side, they sure aren't going to give it up to you."

He knelt beside her and grabbed her chin. "Adam will see to it that they are agreeable."

Her broken cheek throbbed in his grasp, but she smiled through the pain. He thought that to save her, Adam would help him take over Chuparosa. As if he could even if he wanted to, even if she would let him do that for her.

She recoiled as something brown and withered that hung around Walter's neck fell across her face.

"You like this?" He held it out and scratched her skin with its rough sides.

"What is it?"

He jerked one of the other vampires out of his seat and flopped down on the threadbare couch.

"The vampires came from the old world on the boats. You see, they bought the same lie that I did."

"Lie?"

"Roanoke Colony was supposed to be our chance for freedom. Our salvation. Our gateway to greatness." He held up his hands prayerlike to the ceiling. "They told us gold and treasure lay scattered along the beaches, but they didn't tell us about the freezing winter and the starvation." He lowered his hands and made fists with them. "They didn't tell us about the Indians and that they would have just as soon kept their land for themselves."

"And the Indians surely didn't tell us about the vampires in the woods." He poked a finger in her chest. "It's true I never went to school, but I doubt they printed any of *those* stories in the history books."

"When the blood suckers came for me, I couldn't fight them off, though I surely tried." His red eyes hardened, and Cara finally saw through the blistered skin that they were a washed out blue.

"There was a rotund beauty among them who took pity and gave me her blood, but then she disappeared. When I woke up the wolves were chewing on my legs. Do you know that wolf blood tastes like a good dark ale?" He knelt at her side again, waving the ear. "I'll bet you were spicy; did you burn Adam's tongue when he made you?"

She kicked at him, and the effort took the last of her strength. She heard him laugh as her consciousness faded–that low, sickening laugh. Then she heard him spit on the floor in front of her.

Even under the worst of conditions, Cara would always be an early riser, though it took some time to convince her swollen eyelids to open that evening. She could not see Walter or Betty, but the others were still sleeping, sprawled wherever they'd found space on the floor. Her mind was fuzzy but racing. What could she do with that precious time?

She shifted her body to find a more comfortable position but felt, of all things, her cell phone bulging against her hip in her pocket. Walter didn't understand the technology and probably never even thought to take it from her.

Painful as it was, she maneuvered herself around until it fell out, hitting the wood floor with what sounded to her like a deafening crash. She rolled on top of it and squeezed her eyes closed, waiting for the inevitable punishment to come. After a few seconds passed, she opened them again, and remarkably, no one had heard.

Her hands were numb and blue from lack of circulation, but she slowly worked her fingers around and used her thumbprint to unlock the phone. As she feared, her rustling had disturbed the others and they began to stir. Still, before anyone noticed, she managed to send a location ping to the only person in the world who would know exactly what to do.

Chapter Twenty

A blast of cold air from their twentieth century refrigerator hit Laura in the face when she opened the top freezer door. Bash refused to get rid of it, regardless of how much more efficient the new ones were. She had once tried to explain that their bills would be lower but gave up when he argued, "But it came with the house."

Bash loved everything about their little Santa Fe style home from the Kiva fireplace to, apparently, the rust-colored fridge. She couldn't believe the previous owners had even found a rust-colored refrigerator and told herself that it must be one of a kind and therefore worth keeping, even as their electric bill soared in July.

To his credit, Bash's love of old things and his ability to keep them running was a big part of why they were able to live so comfortably, and she had to admit that blast of cold air had been a welcome relief during the summer.

Before meeting Bash, she started meal prepping as a single mom who worked full time but continued the practice even after she retired and Brian went away to college. First, out of habit and then after realizing that Heaven's Watch was frequently in need of a quick, hearty meal on the run, for example, up to Pinetop to hunt some vampires. Her freezer was always packed and since there would be four of them going up north, she selected large containers of chicken and rice soup and chipotle shredded beef.

She threw in a can of biscuits, a package of tortillas, some shredded cheese, and a jar of homemade salsa. While reaching for a bowl of salad in the crisper, she remembered what they were planning to do and abandoned it for a morale building option. There were three bags of Doritos in the pantry and since Bash had no off switch when it came to chips, she grabbed two, then added what was left of a six pack and a bottle of wine to the cooler and closed the lid.

Since they were fond of picnicking, they kept a drawstring bag pre-loaded with paper plates, utensils and napkins hanging on a hook inside the pantry door. As she dug around inside of it to see what restocking needed to be done, there was a knock at the door. A peaceful feeling fell over Laura, as if someone had draped her in a comfortable old quilt, soft and enduring.

"Come on in Rhonda!"

Since they were in high school, Rhonda DeSchene had been there for Laura and Sarah as a mentor, a stand-in mother, and the dearest of friends. Being in her late sixties, Rhonda had begun to move a bit slower, but not so slow that her gait was any less determined, particularly when she was irritated with one of them.

"You've lost your mind this time," she snapped, stepping past Laura.

"I would second that, but I know better than to try

and talk you out of it," Sarah huffed, following her inside, loaded down with bags.

Rhonda was addicted to the cheap cloth shopping bags handed out by specialty shops and she had one dedicated to each spell they had discussed. Assigning intention to an ingredient was tricky business and she preferred to keep them separated. Depending on their goals, with the same herb they could give a man the sensation of soaring through the air or they could cause him erectile dysfunction—one must be cautious.

Rhonda would repeat those lessons over and over until the day she died, but she would not waste any more time lecturing Laura about the lunacy of going after vampires. She was pleased that she and Sarah still went to her for advice and was determined to give them her best.

Laura and Sarah were unmatched locally in their ability to wield the elements, but Rhonda's unfortunate history with an abusive husband had led her to investigate the subtleties of baneful spellcasting that until recently the Deanes had little use for.

"I'm not interested in playing it safe out there and survival of the intended mark, be it a vampire or an angel, is not a concern," Laura said while relieving Sarah of her load, "and we don't have much time."

Sarah snatched the last bag of Doritos from the open pantry and tore it open. "Of course we don't," she mumbled with her mouth full. "What did you have in mind?"

Laura plucked a tiny tin man from the windowsill over the sink and twirled it between her fingers. The tin man had been part of her mother's Wizard of Oz collection, and it was the only thing of hers that Laura kept after she died.

"Did you bring the book?" she asked Sarah.

Though their mother, Brona Deane, had renounced witchcraft later in life, she was a powerful practitioner as a young adult. Brona had even summoned Thomas, the fallen angel who demanded that she give him children as payment for his services. Her spell book was full of hexes, charms and curses that under normal circumstances they would hesitate to even read aloud; but since joining Heavens Watch, they were less inclined to write them off.

"Are you sure about this?" Sarah intended her words to be cautionary, but her eyes twinkled with excitement as she rifled through her purse for the book.

Typically, Laura reworked her mother's spells with an eye toward self-defense but that night she studied the work as her unstable mother would have—intent on a vicious attack.

They spread a black linen cloth over the round patio table out back and dropped resin incense onto a charcoal briquet that smoldered in a tera cotta pot at the center of the table. A thick salt circle was formed around the entire back porch and sprinkled with rosemary needles, then they lit black pillar candles every two feet along the flagstone border. It was a solid boundary, but dangerous spirits would be drawn to such dark workings so Watson patrolled the perimeter to protect his Laura from those beings that only a hellhound could see.

"With the right dosage," Rhonda began, "this potion will cause restlessness, loss of focus and more importantly for our purposes, hallucinations." She tossed three boxes of sea sickness pills on the table. "It's also easily absorbed by the skin."

Sarah gave her sister a look and said, "Imagine the possibilities."

They dissolved the pills with belladonna in a saucepan over the grill, and Rhonda dropped in few sugar cubes saturated with LSD.

"You better not tell the sheriff," she teased. As if Bash would be surprised that she'd been experimenting with illegal drugs *medicinally* since the seventies.

They added gelatin to the pot and then spread the mixture on a sheet of waxed paper. When cool it was cut into squares and stacked between pieces of scrapbook paper left over from Halloween. The paper was printed with little skulls and selected both to be humorous and to warn anyone else in their party of its dangers.

"Don't get it on you," Sarah warned.

"The trick will be getting close enough to put it on a vampire," Laura said, filing the deadly little packet into her ever-present magical medicine bag.

Sarah had a feeling that wasn't going to be a problem and her stomach turned with fear for her sister. Without looking up from their mother's book, she asked, "Are we not going to talk about Lucifer's deal with those idiots?"

Laura very much wanted to talk about Bash and Drew's unwitting agreement to work with Hell, but it would have to wait. Bash would be back soon with Adam, and they were running out of time.

"Lucifer is not part of Adam's mess," Laura reminded her.

"Yeah, but he sure wants it cleaned up in a hurry."

Laura did her best Scarlet O'Hara impression,

tossing back her curls and drawling, "I'll think about that tomorrow."

"Should we tell Thomas?"

"Did daddy dearest leave *you* his celestial cell number because I sure don't have it."

"Focus on what you can control right now," Rhonda advised.

"Let's find Cara," Laura sighed, "Adam thinks she's off doing superhero things, but I have my doubts."

"Right." Sarah flipped through the pages for the right combination of correspondences. Brona was always looking for things but for nothing as prosaic as her keys or wallet. She searched for specific places in Chuparosa and had even drawn up a map of various portals and pathways she'd discovered in town. Laura and Sarah planned to investigate each of those someday, but at the time they were more interested in Brona's methods.

Cara and Adam had given Laura an antique powder compact for her birthday, which she placed in the middle of the table atop a silk scarf Cara left in Laura's Jeep.

The hope was that Cara's essence on the items would be enough to conjure her whereabouts, but then Laura said, "look at this," and collected three strands of long, expensively blonde hair from the folds of the scarf. They burned the hair with the incense and together recited Brona's words while Laura fastened the scarf around her neck.

"You ready baby? Adam's meeting us at the sta—" Bash stopped at the back door. He was familiar with a certain crackle in the air after Laura worked a spell, but what lingered outside had a sharper edge to it than he was used to.

"Christ, what have you three been doing?"

"Relax and have a snack honey," Rhonda patted his belly and handed him Sarah's bag of chips. "We're just taking some extra precautions."

Indeed, Bash was awash in defenses as he inadvertently stepped into their circle. Dark as it was, the magic gave him a weird sense of security, if not a sense of comfort. In that he was not alone for Watson nudged at his hips, even happier to have him home than he was to be sharing his Doritos.

Rhonda pulled Laura aside while the others gathered up the materials.

"Look at you," she said with a huff, "on your way to fight monsters most people only meet in their nightmares and you're not taking care of yourself, girl."

She wrapped a leather cord beaded with garnet and turquoise around Laura's wrist. Rhonda had fashioned a more delicate version of the shield bracelets Laura once made for Bash and Drew. Delicate, but no less powerful. Laura's head jerked up as the magnetic clasp fastened and a current shot through her body.

"Rhonda!" she gasped. It must have taken everything out of the older woman to create such a talisman and Laura was torn between gratitude and annoyance that she's spent so many of her precious reserves on it.

Rhonda waved a dismissive hand and said, "I was put here in part to raise up you and your sister and you've made me so proud that I intend to do it for the rest of my life."

Tears jumped to Laura's eyes, and she wrapped Rhonda in a tight hug. She had the sudden knowledge that their time together was short but could not sort out her feelings enough to tell her everything she needed to say.

In her heart Laura knew it was not the old woman's days that were numbered, and Rhonda knew it too. She pulled away and touched their foreheads together, leaving Laura with a knowing look that would haunt her upon their return.

Rhonda and Sarah kicked off their shoes and walked barefoot in the dirt to release the residual energy they'd gathered. The three hour drive up north would be excruciating, but Laura could not afford to get rid of any stored power, so she staggered inside to find Bash. He gave her new bracelet a twist and then gave her a worried look.

She stood on tiptoe and kissed his nose. "Just load the Jeep and then we'll talk about it while I do my nails."

She waved her fingers at him and went to the bedroom. Laura couldn't make fire, her power was in her ability to manipulate it. In the past she could only work with whatever flames were available, but the phosphorescent nail polish she'd come up with now kept the element literally at her fingertips. While it wasn't a foolproof solution, any number of wicked things had paid the price for doubting her.

Bash hoisted the cooler off the kitchen table, knowing full well they would not have a chance to talk about it, and for once he was fine with that. A familiar but detested fear was creeping back into his bones and his faith in her abilities was much stronger than in his own.

Chapter Twenty-One

"You numbskulls dragged me into work after dinner to help you pack for vampire hunting?" Billy Tate's voice was harsh when he pushed through the glass door of the Sheriff's station, but his steel gray eyes were clouded with concern. "Bash, I believe this is the dumbest shit you've done yet."

Billy worked the desk so Chuck and Bash could see to the dehydrated tourists, the meth labs, and the wife beaters in town without worrying about what was happening back at the office–and there was always something happening. Ostensibly they did call him that night to help but the truth was that for all his cantankerous blustering they were comforted by his presence. Billy had raised six boys over the course of his lifetime and only a few of them were his own.

It would be fair to think that being in his seventies, he would have earned the right to relax; but, if you'd mentioned that to him, he would have told you to fuck all the way off.

Though the fatherless Sebastian Scott was a more

recent acquisition, he considered the middle-aged deputy sheriff to be his seventh son and treated him accordingly, that is, with more love and more harshly than he treated anyone else in the room.

Bash ignored his commentary. "Help me set up those new two-way radios, will you?"

"For vampires?" Billy huffed. "You gonna call 'em names?"

"Billy...god dammit."

Few others would have seen it, but Billy took note of the slight tremble in Bash's hands and that the swagger had gone out of his stride. He retrieved two shotguns from the gear rack on the wall and said, "Alright, load these, and I'll go find your techy crap."

He'd given his boys many different pep talks over the years but understandably didn't have one in the can about how most men would straight up piss themselves at the thought of what Bash and his friends had been doing for the last year. A bit of a tremor was to be expected when there was the possibility of getting your throat torn out, but Bash would never accept that.

He entered the storage room hearing a clatter and a curse as Bash fumbled the box, rolling shotgun shells off the table in every direction, so he turned on his heel, ready to wing it.

"Fuck me," Bash growled under his breath, bending to pick up the shells.

Though he'd gotten skinny in his old age, at six foot five, Billy was the only one in town who could rival Bash in height. Placing a firm hand around the younger man's bicep, he straightened to his full stature.

"Let 'em go," he ordered, "and take a breath."

Bash ran a hand through his hair and heaved a sigh,

which wasn't exactly what Billy had in mind, but he released his arm and said, "You're the bravest man I've ever known. I give you the most shit because you have to think the hardest about what you're gonna do."

Looking down at his hands, Bash opened and closed his fists a few times. He laughed to keep the panic out of his voice when he argued, "I'm not very brave tonight."

"Look at me, boy." Billy waited until Bash met his eyes and said, "You are especially brave tonight."

Chuck's voice in the background as he spoke on the phone, and Laura's rummaging through the storage room sounded so distant to both men that they could have been underwater. A full thirty seconds passed while Bash soaked in Billy's words and then a loud rumble outside shook them out of their concentration.

Billy worried that he might not have gotten through, but Bash squared his shoulders, racked the slide on a shotgun and aimed it at the door. "Get behind me," he commanded.

"No need for that." Sam's deep voice echoed through the room before he stepped inside, followed by Adam and Carl. Before they could trade insults, Chuck hung up the phone and pulled up the internet browser on his computer.

He was still moving slowly but his color had improved quite a bit. Bash wondered if the poison had truly dissipated on its own or if Lucifer had something to do with Chuck's recovery. As he watched his friend back in action, more or less, he found that he didn't really care what the answer was.

"Doug and Angie will meet you at the cabin, and this thing," Chuck waved his hand over the monitor, "says they're gettin' snow in Pinetop, but Doug said it's sleet so be careful. You got chains for the Jeep?"

"No need for that either." Sam dangled a set of keys in front of them. "We got a Hummer."

"A what?" Laura had taken it upon herself to hide out in the storage room while Billy worked some of his own style of magic on Bash's mental state. She plopped a box down on Bash's desk and said, "Here's the radios and the last of the ammo that Daniel blessed for you."

"Niiiice," Sam drawled, looking her over. He eyed the tactical way in which she was dressed and turned to Bash for confirmation. "We're bringing the A-Team?"

"To the cabin," Adam clarified. He could see the value in having her standing by up there, but he would never let her risk her life beyond that–not for him.

Bash gave Sam a sideways glance. He didn't have the energy to explain to Adam that he and Laura were a package deal, all the way to Hell if necessary.

Laura leveled her gaze on Adam. "I'm going wherever Bash goes," she said coolly.

"You are not going all the way out there with us," Adam argued.

"Yes I am."

"No, no. Tell her Sebastian," he pleaded, "tell her why she can't go."

"Adam," Bash rubbed at his goatee, "we're gonna need Laura's power."

"Don't you understand?" Adam took Laura's face in his hands. "They'll do things to you that you can't even—"

"I have to go," she interrupted, "because you won't be able to deal with Walter and Cara at the same time."

Adam blinked at her. He hadn't thought of that.

"I don't know if Cara's working with him or not, but I know what she's capable of and you won't be able to do what it takes to stop her."

"And you will?"

"I've done it before." Laura was no dainty little thing, but just then she felt very small, the only woman in a room full of enormous men who had suddenly turned all eyes on her. Men whose perceived power over her actions made her vulnerable in their eyes and thus in her own. It frightened her and she had to remind herself that they were as large in compassion and character as they were in stature and strength.

Still, she needed them to make no mistake about what the women in their lives could bring to the table, both good and bad. She lifted her chin and squared her shoulders, taking up as much space as her five foot ten inches would allow and said, "You like to think that you're the devil Adam, that no one else could do the things you're willing to do to survive, but I'll bet I could give you a run for your money."

Chapter Twenty-Two

To a man, their faces displayed disbelief and dismissal, her fury at this giving her the courage to add, "Cara nearly killed Brian's father. And I nearly let her."

"Baby..."

She backed away when Bash reached for her. If she went to him, she would bury her head in his chest, and he would let that be the end of it. Her short revelation was enough of a warning, but they needed to hear it, and she needed to tell the secret she'd kept for almost twenty-two years.

Having garnered their unwavering attention, she continued, "I don't want to accidentally manifest him by saying his name, but when Brian's father abandoned us, we were better for it." She looked down. "He wasn't some kind of self-aware rambler who decided to do us a favor and disappear. We *made* it happen, Cara and me."

When Bash met Laura, she'd offered little more than a brief summation of how Brian's father left her. He assumed she wasn't in the ex-ranting business, particularly since Brian was grown, and since that guy's loss was his gain, Bash never pressed her for more information. *Don't ask questions you don't want the answers to.*

But Laura stared out the window that night and gave them all the answers, whether they wanted them or not.

They didn't date for very long. He had a mean, controlling streak and Laura thought she'd escaped him, but some weeks after they broke up, she found out that she was pregnant.

"He was furious and accused me of trying to trap him and ruin his life. I couldn't stand the idea of spending forever with him, but I thought it was only fair to tell him about the baby," She clarified, "I specifically said I didn't want anything from him."

"He disappeared for a while but then called me out of the blue when Brian was about four weeks old, raving about child support. Again, I told him I didn't want it, but a friend of his apparently warned him that I could sue for back support even after Brian turned eighteen. He was a successful website builder, but his company was small, and he thought I would try to take everything from him."

"I offered to sign some kind of waiver, but he said that wasn't good enough. He said he was going to make sure I didn't try anything stupid, but I didn't take him seriously enough."

Laura could remember every detail of the night Brian's father attacked. After working late, she raced to daycare and to the store because she'd invited Chuck's wife Mena, her sister, and Cara over to drink wine and watch Jerry Maguire.

After putting away the groceries, her heart stopped when she closed the refrigerator to find him standing on the other side of the door with Brian in his arms.

"I'm going to show you what will happen if you try to take me to court," he threatened.

After a lifetime of experience in law enforcement, Bash, Chuck and Sam knew what she would say next, and that they would be furious, but they remained silent and let her tell it.

Laura could have attacked him with fire from the stove but didn't want to hurt the baby or burn down her house, so she attacked him with her fists. He dropped Brian in the sink, grabbed her arms and kneed her in the belly.

"I kicked and scratched and fought, but I was young. I didn't have the skill or the control over my powers that I have now, and he had caught me off guard."

Verbalizing the scenario made her acutely aware that for years she'd been more angry with *herself* for the attack than she was at Brian's father. She laughed inwardly as she suddenly realized that the need to make excuses for not being able to fight off a violent man at any time, let alone weeks after giving birth was absurd.

Bash could taste the blood from where he'd been biting down on the inside of his cheek, and he was glad she wouldn't say the man's name. He'd never be able to promise her that he wouldn't go looking for him.

Laura said, "All of a sudden, he screamed and doubled over against the sink. I looked up and Cara was standing there with a baseball bat in her hands. She would have swung again, but he put Brian under his arm and ran out of the house."

Laura had to move slowly but they followed the baby's cries into the desert, down a deep wash where he had stuffed Brian in a small hollow. He stood in front of it with his arms crossed, daring them to approach him.

"I obviously couldn't fight him, so I pulled some fire from a lighter in my pocket and threw it at his feet. He reached for Brian, and I was terrified of what he might do, but the stems from a young Ocotillo stretched out to make a little gate of thorns over the hollow."

As an aside for Sam's benefit, Billy explained, "Chuparosa takes care of its own." Though he thought in that case, it could have acted a little sooner.

"Yeah, but he was pretty pissed." Laura sniffed. "I doubt anyone had ever stood up to him in his life." She absently rubbed her hands together and passed thin blue strands of electricity between her fingers as she continued the story.

"I pulled every bit of fuel from that little lighter and made a wall between him and the baby. Then he really screwed up."

When Brian's father shrank away from the flames, Cara swung the bat across his shoulders and when he collapsed, she kicked him headfirst into the fire.

"I moved the flames away before he was any more than singed, but he writhed around as if we'd dipped him in lava." She rolled her eyes. "Then Brian started screaming and it was like Cara went into a trance. She held the bat high, ready to bring it down on his head."

"I had to force myself to make her stop." Laura confessed, "Cara was so full of rage that she wouldn't even look at me. Adam, did she ever tell you how she got that scar on her right arm?"

He shook his head.

"No? Well, it was me. I had to move the fire wall between her and Brian's dad. She still wouldn't put the bat down, so I inched the flames so close that she had to shield her face with her arms. She wouldn't move away until she was burned."

"I wasn't going to let her ruin her life over a man like him," Laura finally looked up at them, "even though I wanted nothing more than for her to do just that."

Bash would not keep his distance any longer. He wrapped his arms around her waist, murmuring his support in her ear. She leaned back into his chest but kept her eyes on Adam.

"When you made Cara a vampire," she said, "you gave her the power and the permission to go after all the bad men. I don't care about them, but I do care about her."

"What ever happened to your baby daddy?" If they didn't kill him, Sam wondered what in the hell they *did* do to him.

"He passed out from the shock, so I worked a spell to make him forget all about us," she said. "Then we parked him and his car on a dirt road somewhere in Avondale. I look him up on the Internet every now and then to make sure, but he's fine. He sold his company and moved to Colorado, and I haven't heard from him since that night."

"Heh, heh, heh," Billy chuckled, "You chose well Bash," he said under his breath. "That woman will keep your blood pressure runnin' high, but you chose well."

Adam would second that notion and Laura was right. It killed him to admit it, but if Cara was involved, he could not be sure if she was a prisoner or an accomplice. He hated putting her in that position, but Laura's help would be invaluable.

Telling her secrets had left her feeling vulnerable and exposed but she'd made her point. Unwilling to dwell on it after receiving Adam's reluctant acceptance, she busied herself by filling a backpack with the radio equipment.

"Give me a minute." Sam jogged out to the Hummer and returned with what looked like a black cell phone box. "I'll see your fancy radios and raise you a stun gun that doubles as a flashlight."

He plucked a pair of scissors from a cup on the desk to snip the zip ties from around the box, but his thumb twisted in the handle ring, curling his wrist downward in an unnatural, painful looking pose.

"What the hell?"

Laura made a show of putting the scissors in his other hand and said, "These are Sebastian's left-handed scissors."

"Jesus," Sam put down the scissors and fished out a pocketknife, "I thought I was havin' a stroke." He popped open the box and held up the flashlight, pressing a red button on the side to demonstrate its tasing capabilities. "It even has a lighter at the bottom." He winked at Laura, turned it over and flicked the spark wheel, igniting a small flame that she pulled across the desk into her palm.

"Handy," she admitted.

He gave her beltloop a tug, drawing her close to him so he could clip it to her pants. "I got all the good toys, sweetheart." He turned to face Adam. "And, I've got some related news. Our Miss Cara might be hot to kill abusers, but I don't think she's gone all the way to the dark side yet."

"Turns out there was a survivor at the Glendale warehouse. He said that before the vampire killed his girlfriend, another vampire tried to stop her, and that vampire's name was Cara."

They all stopped to look at him.

"As you can imagine, the guy was pretty traumatized and couldn't remember hearing the first vampire's name, but he has a sister named Cara so that one stuck with him. It don't matter though because he gave us something almost as good as a name."

"What's *almost* as good?" Laura wondered.

"He said the killer had lavender colored hair." He turned to Bash and said, "That means purple."

Bash curled his lip, but before he could comment, Adam said, "We know the other vampire is in Pinetop. If Cara is with her then she's also with Walter." His voice was hard, but his expression could not hide the breaking of his heart.

"We also know that Cara was trying to stop her," Chuck reminded him.

"We'll find her, and we might even make it out alive," Sam snapped Bash's scissors in the air, "in spite of your disability."

"Hey Chuck," Billy called out from the window, "if you put in a requisition for one of those Hummers, we could retire that embarrassing piece of shit you drive around."

Chuck made a face. "That hummer costs more than this building."

Laura didn't trust Sam or his vehicle or even his motives for that matter. Still, she'd never liked the idea of a convoy up north, and even if Sam was insufferable about it, the Hummer would keep them together, transporting the four of them, the dogs, their gear, and hopefully at some point, Cara.

She tuned out their banter when her phone made a strange noise. The notification was from a feature that, living in a small town, she didn't use very often, and it took her a minute to realize what she was looking at. It was a ping. A location ping from Cara's number.

Chapter Twenty-Three

Carl sat forward from the cargo space with his chin on the back seat, so Bash reached around to give Adam's dog a comforting scratch behind the ears. Laura did the same for him, sliding her fingers up his neck and into his hair. She massaged the back of his head until his shoulders inched away from his ears. The mountains in the Tonto Forest loomed large and the darkness threatened to swallow them up as Sam wove the Hummer around the sharp curves in the road.

Adam gazed onto Highway 87 from the window of the front passenger seat sensing the tired tension in the others. Though he felt that Sam could slow to at least sixty on the turns, the gloom of the scenery had been his desert experience for over a hundred years, and the sights invigorated him as he contemplated the final end, one way or another, to the scourge that was Walter.

He'd seen Walter last in the early eighties and it would have ended then if not for the advances made in security. It was a heady time for Arizona and for Adam, who'd become a successful electrician capitalizing on the booming development in the east valley.

1986

On weekends Adam spent his evenings in dimly lit country bars two-stepping with his friends to Roseanne Cash, Eddie Rabbit, and Alabama. The farmers, cowboys, and construction workers he hung out with preferred dollar drafts and darts to the cover charges, laser lights and pop music in the Scottsdale clubs.

It was rare, but since he'd been turned there were occasions when he would indulge in bouts of self-pity that could last anywhere from an hour to several months. During one such episode he used money from his fast-filling bank account to buy a new record player from which Kris Kristofferson's regret filled lyrics filled his room on repeat. Peeking around blackout curtains to watch yet another sunrise from a safe distance, the dull ache of loneliness settled around his heart.

He cast a glance at his empty bed and then scratched the needle across the record. Kris's words resonated a little too well and brooding over it was giving him an ugly mean feeling.

He'd been talked into a date with a friend of a friend who had tickets to see the Kinks at Club Rio. Though it wasn't his usual scene, he accepted the date with hopes that they might hit it off. Hopes that were quickly dashed when she ran into a friend mid-show who took her backstage to meet the band.

Adam didn't blame her since it turned out that she was quite a bit younger than he'd been led to believe. She was kind to him and did her best, but he was sure that she was planning to kill their mutual friend who'd set her up with an 'old man'. He'd had a good laugh about that–she had no idea.

He stayed for the rest of the show, which was better than he expected, and then decided to take the river walk home. As he approached Tempe Beach Park on the bank of the Salt River, a man perched atop the back of a bench called out to him, "Got a light?"

Assuming he was a drunk, Adam ignored him and kept walking but, from the corner of his eye he saw the man spit tobacco and get up to follow him toward the water. The man trotted to catch up until they were walking side by side and, in the glow of the streetlights Adam caught site of the red, peeling skin around his eyes and whirled on his maker. He'd fantasized about killing Walter so many times that his actual presence seemed almost intrusive, but Adam was more than ready.

"What do you want?" The bitter feelings he'd tried so hard to quash earlier that day flooded into the fists curling at his sides.

Walter waved his hand from Adam's head to his feet. "Look at you trying to act like you belong," he mocked him. "You got the clothes and the hair, but you don't fit in any more than I do." Walter wore blue jeans—he still tucked them into his boots, a collarless button-down shirt and a pork pie hat similar to the one he had always worn. But for the missing filth, he could have just stepped out of the mine.

Though he didn't have much in the way of personal style himself, Adam got a kick out of the evolving fashions and had even worn parachute pants that night to the concert.

"I'm just living my life. You didn't give me much of

a choice, did you?" he seethed.

One thing Adam had learned during their confrontations over the years is that Walter was opposed to anything that resembled assimilation. He didn't even put much energy into their fights, it was more of a game to him. One he didn't seem to care if he won or lost.

"No one gets a choice." Walter spit again. "When I came west to the desert," he held his arms out wide, "there was so much space that people could never fill it up. But they sure did."

"I know. I was there." Adam was losing his patience, though Walter's motives became clearer with each meeting. Had the vampires not come for him, Adam wondered if Walter would have survived his first year in the 'new world'. He could not have adapted to times as they changed back then any more than he could in a world with microwave ovens. Adam had no love for the fast pace of modern life, but where he'd formed connections and learned to appreciate its comforts, Walter had simply become feral.

Adam's eyes darted to the small group of people milling around on the beach and said, "If you want to fight, then let's go somewhere else and end this."

With speed Adam hadn't seen in years, Walter reached out and took him by the throat. "You want one of them first?" Walter tightened his grip, amused by Adam's concern for the bystanders.

Fighting in the open like that would not only risk the lives of those people, but his hard-won lifestyle as well. He had to get away, so he wrapped his hands around the back of Walter's head and pressed his thumbs into his eyes.

Walter staggered back and, as Adam feared, roared in pain, attracting the attention of the beach goers who wisely chose to move along without asking any questions.

Adam charged at his middle and knocked Walter down. Hovering over him, he rubbed his throat, rasping, "If you hate life so much, why don't you just take a walk in the sun?"

Walter rolled onto his side and pressed himself up, wiping the blood from his cheeks with the back of his hand. "If you think there's relief in a death like that, you should try it."

The realization sank in. Apparently, Walter had done just that. Adam studied the blisters around his eyes for a moment and wondered how long he'd lasted before giving up. Of course, he too was afraid to die screaming as the flesh melted off his bones, but at some point, Walter had gotten a taste of what that might be like for real.

Still, rather than working within the confines of his affliction to build himself a better life, Walter afflicted himself on others, determined to be a force for revenge and suffering until he did finally meet his end.

Adam was happy to oblige his death wish. Ready to pounce, he crouched down and lowered his fangs just as Walter kicked out and swept his legs from underneath him. He leapt to the side, splashing in the shallows before Walter could pin him down. He advanced on him, forcing them both knee deep into the river and then Walter caught him in the chin with an upper cut. The water rushed over his face and again, he felt that iron grip around his throat as Walter knelt over him. He forced a knee into his groin and as he fell backward, Adam rose up choking for air but also throwing a wild haymaker into Walter's jaw. When the older vampire went down, Adam sprang atop his chest and slammed his head down over and over on the rocks until his body went slack.

Scanning the beach, he spotted a wooden bench. He plodded toward it and as he yanked a slat from the seat, a voice yelled, "Hey!"

Adam looked up to see a park ranger headed his way with a flashlight and a drawn gun. *Shit.*

"Don't fucking move," the ranger warned.

Adam winced as the ranger shined the flashlight in his face and searched him for weapons. "I fell in," he said weakly, glancing behind him toward the river.

The ranger snatched the bench slat away from him and tossed it to the side. He studied Adam's injuries and noted the blood on his shirt, not quite believing that it was just a fall. "Well, you can't use the bench to build a fire. Are you drunk?"

Adam shrugged and staggered a bit, leaning into the accusation.

"Do you need medical attention?"

"No."

"Then get out of here. The park is closing."

The ranger marched him out and when they reached the gate, Adam stared back wistfully at Walter's body as it floated away with the current.

Chapter Twenty-Four

Present Day

The rough scrape of Walter's knife whittled away at Betty's nerves as roughly as it did the piece of pine he'd plucked from the wood box. Of course, it could have been because she'd felt the scrape of that knife against her body on occasion, but she preferred to think that it was Walter's incessant adherence to the old ways that drove her mad. He could sit there for hours without a thought in his head except for the small woodland creature that would inevitably emerge from the shavings.

The little hunter's shack was closing in on her and Betty began to pace back and forth like a caged animal. A blister was forming on the back of her heel, rubbed by the oversized stolen boots. She pulled at the excess wool slouched near the back of the boot and made a face at the disappointing sock technology.

She might have sought solidarity with the other woman in the room, but Cara's unconscious body lay motionless on the floor, her pale skin nearly translucent and her hair thin and brittle from lack of nourishment.

How long was it going to take for Adam to find them? It was possible that Cara was telling the truth, and he didn't care about her, but Betty was doubtful. She'd seen them together and while their interactions were tense; he'd gazed at Cara with that look. The slight crinkle between his brows indicated that he had no idea what to do about their problems, but it was coupled with a determined flash in his eyes that said he would try anything to make her happy. It was a look he'd given Betty only once. Once, before she...

Oh well. Jess Carson was long gone, and Adam was either over it or he wasn't. They would find out soon enough. No matter how pissed he was at Cara, if she died, Betty would never be forgiven. Of that she was certain, and she had to be forgiven.

Walter thought Adam was afraid of him, but the only thing Adam Colter feared was losing the people he loved. Cara was right and he would never turn over his town, his precious Chuparosa. He was going to kill Walter. Of that she was also certain, so for the time being, saving Cara was her priority. There would be plenty of opportunities to get rid of her later.

Betty nudged the cooler open with the toe of her boot to find that Walter's men had emptied it out. They even ate the candy bar she'd hidden at the bottom.

"Did you see this?" She glared at Walter's back. "Your gaggle of idiots has eaten everything we brought."

"Won't hurt you none to miss a meal," he said.

She stalked around the kitchen, tossing the saucepan in the sink and the coffee pot after it.

Walter finally looked up from his work. "Knock off

that noise."

She picked up the remaining walking stick and slammed it over and over against the wall, screeching "I'm. Suffocating. In. Here!" in time with the banging.

He jerked her by the arm and shoved her at one of the *idiots* who had been laughing at her tantrum.

"Take her to town and fill the Jeep with gas."

Betty rubbed her bicep, simpering, "I need some money for food."

Walter ran the blade of his knife under her chin. "You're a clever girl, you'll be fine."

Sulking in the passenger seat as Dave filled up the gas tank, Betty dwelled on Walter's comment about her weight. He called her chubby to compensate for the fact that he was such a small man in so many ways. *Fuck him.* She poked her head out the window and smiled at Dave.

"Go steal me a Snickers," she purred.

"Nah," he said, "I'm gonna get a treat for me."

Betty followed his gaze to a copper-headed woman who left the store twirling an obnoxiously sized key ring around her finger. She was headed to the bathrooms in the back.

"You better hope she's not a screamer." Betty sniffed, adding, "moron," as he hurried away.

She choked as a puff of exhaust wafted over the Jeep and scanned the area for the source of the annoyance. On the other side of the parking lot, a young, stressed-out looking man jumped down from a semi cab. His boots slid out from underneath him, and he had to reach for the door to keep from falling in the snow. He slammed it closed and looked around to see if anyone had noticed, then tucked his chin and tromped inside the store.

Dave waited near a dumpster outside of the bathroom for his redhead to come out but unbeknownst to him, a large black man with a gun was waiting on the other side of it.

"I might not have dinner, but I'm definitely going to get a show," Betty said to herself.

Sam chuckled as Laura came out of the bathroom trying not to gag with her t-shirt over her mouth and nose. Even for a gas station bathroom it must have been awful.

Not that he didn't think she could handle it, but he'd seen the man follow her from the pumps and since Bash and Adam were busy buying coffee, he took it upon himself to stay close. Just in case.

His intuition was rewarded as the man wasted no time in covering her mouth with his hand and dragging her into the shadows of the building. By the time Sam cleared the sidewalk, Laura had pulled the taser from the clip on her beltloop and shoved it against her assailant's ribcage.

"He's a vampire," she hissed.

As Dave fell twitching to his knees, she used her power to move the taser's electricity into a stream that went from her fingers to a noose that tightened around his neck.

"Hold him there." Sam looked around until he found an empty pallet and broke off a wooden slat. He stomped on the side, shearing off enough to make it sharp and Laura jerked on the electricity to throw Dave onto his back. Sam reached overhead and drove the crude stake through his heart, covering them all in a spray of blood. Dave wailed and gnashed his teeth, grasping at the stake with both hands and begging them to pull it out.

"You would have been just as kind to her." Sam leaned on the stake until he felt it split through Dave's back and pierce the dirt underneath him.

Laura studied the dead vampire for a moment. As a woman, she could expect to be attacked in the dark behind a building, but this wasn't a typical predator. If she hadn't been ready with the taser, he would have bitten her before she knew what was happening. It was good practice, but a wake-up call for sure and she was lucky to be alive.

Resting against the dumpster, she wiped her brow and left a blood smear across her forehead that Sam found alarmingly attractive.

"You sure you don't wanna come work for me A-Team?" He smirked.

She took note of the splatter on her shirtsleeves and made a face. It would require another visit to that horrible bathroom. "I'm positive."

When Dave was throttled by Laura's web of blue electricity, Betty clapped her hands and laughed out loud.

"Bra-vo girlfriend!"

She'd leaned halfway out of the Jeep to watch the spectacle unfold behind the store, so curious about the elemental witch that she almost didn't see the two men sprinting toward the scene. As they rounded the corner the big man took the witch's face in his hands and checked her for damage while the other one got the scoop from staker. Her breath caught in her throat as he looked around. It was Adam.

The black man began to make some serious looking phone calls, so she assumed he was law enforcement of some kind, though it was an unusual cop indeed who staked a vampire like it was the most normal thing you could do on a Tuesday night.

They'd improved her circumstances by ridding her of Dave, but the people with Adam were obviously dangerous. She rolled up the tinted window on the Jeep to avoid discovery and considered her options. She wanted so badly to run to Adam, but he wouldn't trust her, and he would ask about Cara. She caught sight of the clumsy young truck driver paying for his snacks in the store and smiled.

"Yes Walter," she said to herself, "I am a clever girl," and made her way across the parking lot into the back of the trucker's cab.

When the trucker blacked out, hunched over the wheel a few minutes later, she took a KitKat from his bag of snacks. *Finally*, she thought, closing her eyes to savor it. His blood had tasted like tart cherries, and it was a surprisingly good combination.

Chapter Twenty-Five

It was a bad idea to take the job. He'd known it before he left the shipping yard; but Rance Richards had also known that rent and child support were due on the same, rapidly approaching, day. His ex-girlfriend could criticize his ability to communicate, but she could never say that he let his little boy down.

With a fairly new commercial driver's license in his wallet, the twenty-five-year-old had agreed to run a last-minute load up to Pinetop knowing damn well that the icy road conditions were above his skill level. Still, the extra three thousand dollars was going to pay off his Christmas bills and he'd start the new year in the black. For once.

After white knuckling it all the way through the mountains, the stop at Circle K was more to calm his nerves than to fill up with gas. While browsing the aisles for sugar, he overheard a fellow trucker tell the cashier about a skid he nearly didn't make it out of and Rance felt a little boost in his confidence. He'd been lucky, but he'd also done a good job on the road, and he only had a few more miles to go.

He climbed into the cab with a much-improved outlook, anxious to drop the load and get some sleep. The lady's fangs flashed in his peripheral vision and before the instinct to run had even kicked in, she had him straddled and pinned to the seat. He squeezed his eyes closed, and when he opened them, she was gone.

He blinked a few times and as his eyes adjusted to the darkness, sheets of grainy white snow blew sideways out the window. It whipped against the vehicle as if someone were tossing tiny pebbles at the door. For a split second he was grateful not to be on the road since the storm had clearly worsened, but then bewilderment set in. The snow fell at such an odd angle and though he was aware of the throbbing in his head, it was as if the rest of his body had gone numb.

A jolt of panic shot through him as he met resistance while trying to stretch his arms. He would have jerked himself upright, but none of his limbs would move. Confusion dissolved into dread while he twisted against the ropes that hogtied his wrists to his ankles.

And then he remembered it all. He remembered being paralyzed; his face buried in her soft purple hair. He remembered the feel of her tongue on his skin just before she plunged her fangs into his neck.

He wriggled around the tiny space, straining to see in the dark and from what he could tell, she'd left him in the back of a Jeep. Branches heavy with snow scraped the body of the vehicle and he could smell the pines, so for some reason she'd taken him deep into the forest. His imagination ran wild with the possibilities, and he wrestled against the ropes until the last of his strength left him.

Rance had no intention of giving up, but he had no idea what to do and for a long time he laid there winded, terrified, and shivering in the cold.

Though she was nearly blind from withdrawal, her hearing was more acute than ever. Together, the roar of the wind at the cabin door and the crackling of the fire had a hypnotic effect on Cara. They were soothing sounds interrupted by Walter's gruff voice as he snapped at Betty.

"Where's Dave?"

Betty dropped a plastic bag full of chocolate bars and potato chips on the floor next to Cara, who caught the scent of fresh blood in the folds of the handles. Her mind reeled out of focus, her body began to shake, and she knew in her heart that she would not live through the night.

"How the hell should I know?" Betty opened a bag of chips and popped one in her mouth. "I came out of the store, and he was gone," She mumbled. "At least *I'm* loyal."

Walter slapped her. "Stupid bitch."

One of his men went to the window and said, "He can't have gotten far in this mess."

They put on their coats and Walter gave orders for two of the men to search outside the cabin while he and the other one went to town.

"And you," he lifted Betty by the chin until her feet no longer touched the floor, "if you try anything, you're dead." He tossed her across the room and left with his man.

Her body hit the sink before landing with a thud on the wood. "Asshole."

Cara heard the door open and slam shut a few more times, and then there was some rustling and another larger thud next to her. She felt the heat of a body and heard someone exhale with a long groan. She didn't recognize the source, but she did recognize the scent of blood.

She didn't have the strength to lift her head, but she maneuvered her body around enough that she could tell through the haze that it was a man. He'd been beaten and tied up, and the blood she smelled oozed from fresh puncture wounds on his neck.

"I want to call a truce." Betty stood over her and gestured at Rance. "Look, I even brought you a snack."

Cara's mouth watered but she kept still. Rance tried to shrimp away from them, but Betty kicked him in the ribs.

"Don't be like that," she warned him, and then turned her attention back to Cara. "I'm serious," she said. "We're sisters in more ways than you know." She went to the fire and held her hands out to warm them. The tone of her voice became serious, more thoughtful than Cara had ever heard.

"We're in the sisterhood of Adam."

So, it was as Cara suspected. Knowing that there might have been dozens, she had never asked about the women from Adam's past, preferring to focus on their eternal future instead. With some amusement and no small amount of embarrassment, she finally recognized their similarities. Adam's type was small but fiery. Clever, blonde, and vain.

"He never looked at me like I was garbage the way

other men did," Betty said. "They didn't want spinsters. Old hags like me didn't even bother with the matrimonial advertisements of the day. As if those men were worth the cloth my dresses were sewn from." She kicked Rance again on principle.

Betty wasn't as old as Cara when she was turned, but Cara knew firsthand that no matter the century, age was a liability for a woman.

"I suppose it's my own fault," Betty confessed, "because when I had my pick of them, I didn't want one of those dogs. Adam was the exception of course, but I played around with him until it was too late."

Cara found herself angry on Betty's behalf. She was ashamed to admit it, but they were both jealous of the advantages younger women had over those in middle age. Had she not been deathly afraid to face the woman who would haunt her from the mirror if she were *lucky* enough to live another fifty years? She loved Adam but hadn't the ability to avoid further indignities of aging also been one of the driving factors behind why she agreed to let him make her a vampire? Tears welled in her eyes as she again mourned the fact that she and Betty would never be friends.

"I saw Adam in town tonight," Betty said with a sigh. "He was with some cops and a witch."

Laura. Cara breathed an inward sigh of relief. Until then she hadn't allowed herself even the hope that anyone would come for her.

"Witches come in handy," Betty's eyes sparkled with anticipation, "and this one, she's the real deal."

She held out her arms and spun around. "It's thanks to a witch that I'm standing here right now."

"I don't understand what that has to do with me,"

Rance said.

"You may be shocked to learn that not everything is about you." Betty flopped in a chair and crossed her ankles atop his shoulders, making a show of addressing Cara alone.

"Death was everywhere in Bisbee," she explained, "and I knew it was only a matter of time before I felt that pain in my belly. I knew Adam was living there, but I never found him. I found Walter." She crinkled her nose. "He wouldn't turn me though, not even to save my life. He said I was old and burdensome."

"But I'm not stupid. There were quite a few witches in Bisbee at that time, so I got one to show me how to conjure a demon."

"She just showed you?" Cara croaked.

"Well," Betty shrugged, "she had a daughter to protect."

"From you."

Betty rolled her eyes at Cara's lack of vision. "They were digging for copper at the mine, see, but I figured if I could show Walter where the *gold* was, he would change his mind about me, and I was right."

"And you could live forever."

"With only a few wrinkles on this face." She tilted her chin for Rance to admire.

"A demon who finds gold?" he asked.

"Mostly. He does a few other party tricks—earthquakes and the like, but demons are fairly single minded so whenever I come across a witch, I make her teach me her secrets. I know potions of all kinds, but nothing strong enough to rid me of Walter. Lord knows I've tried."

She had tried on several occasions, the punishment

more severe with each failure until she'd given up on the idea all together. Not that the knowledge hadn't proven useful in other ways. Rance's capture being a case in point.

"Anyhoo, after my demon led us to gold in the Chiricahua mountains, Walter kept the only promise he ever made me and turned me into a vampire."

"Why didn't you look for Adam?" It was the one part of Betty's story that Cara didn't understand.

"Walter told me he was dead." Betty's bitterness hung in the air like a poisonous gas. "I didn't find out the truth until a few months ago."

"Walter made you both to suffer along with him," Cara said, "but Adam is thriving."

"He always has, and that drives Walter insane." Betty agreed. "It helps that he was raised right. Did you know that Adam's father was a mountain man?"

Cara had not known that. She was learning that her focus on their future had been a terrible mistake, and she was beyond jealous that Betty knew so many intimate details about him. Details that she herself had simply never cared to ask.

"Was his mother a member of a tribe?"

"You would have thought so." Betty decided not to gatekeep the information, instead quietly delighting in Cara's humiliating ignorance. "Elena was the terribly young widow of a Mexican soldier. They met in Tucson."

"I'll be damned," Cara whispered.

"So would she, according to her father," Betty mused, "for running away with Callum Colter. Adam was their only surviving child."

"My point is," Betty continued, "that Walter wasn't

cut out for thriving. He uses people, hurts them to get what he wants. He's never learned anything except how to be worse. And Adam has come to kill him. He'll do it for you and then we'll all live happily ever after."

Cara shuddered to think about what happily ever after looked like in Betty's world, but hoped for everyone's sake, that she was right.

"He's on his way and Walter will be back soon, so drink up. We don't have much time." Betty scooted Rance's body closer to Cara, positioning his neck near her mouth.

Cara was crazed with desire, but she turned her head away. "I won't hurt him."

Rance decided then that he liked Cara. Liked her very much.

"Suit yourself," Betty sniffed, "but that won't change anything." She went in the bedroom to pack, convinced that Adam would be taking them both back to Chuparosa in a matter of hours.

Rance had listened carefully to their conversation and though he had no idea who the other players were, he did not want to be there when they arrived. He didn't know how Cara had come to be in such a pitiful condition either, but she was his only hope of getting away.

"I'll be killed if you don't," he whispered, "so you might as well."

The tendrils of Cara's depression had loosened a bit, but still she supposed that Adam and her friends would kill the other vampires, not that she would survive.

"She doesn't have to know." Rance could not believe that he was begging a vampire to bite him.

"I don't know if I can stop in time."

He inched closer and whispered, "I'm dead either way."

Chapter Twenty-Six

There was no moonlight that night to reflect off the lake but still the water shimmered as the wind whipped up mini waves that lapped at the ice creeping out from the shore. Chuck's cabin was dark and lacking its usually rustic, welcoming vibe. The surrounding forest cast ominous shadows and the wind blew the branches of the pine trees closest to the cabin so that they scraped against its outer walls.

The group huddled inside the vehicle, weary from the tense drive through the storm. Getting out meant getting on with it and even the dogs didn't seem that eager to face what was ahead of them.

"What's this?" Sam shielded his eyes as a pair of headlights reflected in the side mirror and cut a bright path up the snow-covered road.

The unlikely duo closing in on them consisted of Doug Farmer, a forest management specialist, and his partner Angie Walsh, the author of a popular werewolf romance series. Together, they ran a side business called ButtonTop, managing cabins for owners who didn't live up north full time. Doug and Angie had met under some pretty horrifying circumstances; the kind that made them uniquely qualified to understand the needs of Heaven's Watch.

When Chuck called to warn that the group would be hunting vampires, Doug said simply, "I'll bring the mini excavator," assuming the dead would need to be buried quick and deep.

Angie jumped down from the truck and ran to give Laura a hug. They texted almost daily but hadn't seen each other since Laura's fiftieth birthday party a few months earlier.

"You are rocking middle age," she gushed.

Laura managed a weak smile, feeling that the only thing she rocked at the time was a headache.

"You've got plenty of firewood," Doug assured them, "but I think the wind took out the power."

"I'll take a look," Adam said, already trudging around the house.

Bash laid a hand on Doug's shoulder. "Thanks—I won't forget this." He took in the many windows and stole a glance at Adam by the breaker box, adding, "I guess I never noticed that there aren't any shutters."

"Chuck installed those impact resistant windows that don't need 'em, but I think he stored the old ones in Satan's shed."

"Tell me it ain't really Satan's shed." Sam would not have been surprised if the Devil rented a storage unit from Chuck, but he'd had enough in the way of revelations about that particular deity for the time being.

In fact, the shed was so called because of its eighty's slasher film aesthetic, complete with poisonous insects, rusted tools and dangerous chemicals left behind by the cabin's previous owner. Chuck hadn't made cleaning it out a priority since he and Mena rarely had time to visit their second home and had better things to do when they were up there.

"Hang on." Bash started for the vehicle to unload the gear, but it was empty. He turned in a confused circle to find that Laura and Angie had piled it all by the front door. They were crouched over the woodpile gathering logs to start a fire.

Sam laughed and said, "A-Team."

Doug twisted the key in the shed's padlock and several small, unidentifiable creatures skittered away from the beams of their flashlights.

"Jesus." Sam grimaced as they stepped over a tarantula nest in the doorjamb.

"The power must be out in this whole area." Adam stood at the door of the shed reporting, "Lines are probably down everywhere, but the breaker's not damaged." He frowned, shining his light over the crusty dirt floor. "What the hell is this place?"

"Don't ask," Bash said, handing him some shutters. "Let's put these up and get some food."

The warm glow of the fireplace and the smell of Laura's chipotle beef lowered their blood pressures significantly as the men stepped inside. With their stomachs rumbling, they left their boots by the door and crowded around the stove. Angie and Laura left them to it, lighting more candles and gathering blankets from the bedrooms. They would all have to sleep in the living room to keep warm.

Sam noted Adam freely entering a home that was not his. "So, you can just waltz in here without Chuck's invite?"

Adam had puzzled over the question in the past. "I think it's less about the threshold and more about the protective energy of the home in question. This is not where the Ruiz family lives. It's similar to a hotel in that regard."

Bash was quiet while flipping his tortilla over on the burner. Something hadn't been sitting right with him since he heard Adam's story about Bisbee.

"Why would a gunfighter become a miner?" He asked, handing Adam the package of tortillas. "And don't tell me you just wanted a quiet life."

Not that being a powderman was a safe job, but Bash had never known Adam to shy away from a fight, indeed, it was quite the opposite. "Besides, those mining towns don't sound like they were that quiet."

Adam took a beer from the cooler and settled down with his dinner by the fire. He should have known Bash would sense his half-truth and though that particular story caused him a great deal of pain, he'd lately very much enjoyed reliving his memories of Jess.

"A couple years after Prescott, Jess and I worked a job near Oatman," he began. "A rancher paid us a hell of a lot to handle some of his trouble in town. It was bloody business and lookin' back, he was—and we were—wrong, but there's nothin' I can do about that now." He took a bite and let his eyes roll back in his head. "Delicious, Laura. Anyway, I swear to God Betty Brown could smell money and stupidity from miles away and I was flush with both.

"Stupidity or loneliness?" Laura wondered.

"You give me too much credit." He shook his head, "Betty was bad, bad, bad, but so was I. Jess disagreed, but if ever there were two people who deserved each other..." He finished his burrito and drained his beer. "Against his good advice, we let her ride with us to Flagstaff. As you can imagine she didn't care for the stagecoach anymore and she *said* she wanted to catch the train back east."

Adam's eyes had been dancing in the firelight as he remembered, but just then they turned cold.

"She was so sweet and loving the whole time. You know I actually thought—" he cut himself off and stared into the distance as if he still wondered what could have been.

Flagstaff, Arizona 1883

They hitched their horses to the post outside of the general store just before sundown. The man behind the counter was so engrossed in the newspaper that he didn't look up until Adam piled their purchases on the counter: coffee, jerky, dried strawberries, bullets, and two large, blue and white bandanas.

"You won't believe this," the shop owner showed them an article about something called an arc lamp. Betty yawned as Jess read over Adam's shoulder.

"Would you look at that," Adam mused, "I bet someday there'll be electric lights in every house."

"I'd settle for havin' a house," Jess said, taking a hand mirror from Betty as she tried to shoplift it into her pocket.

"I have money in that bank next door," she told them, "and I need it for my train ticket."

Adam was distracted, fascinated by the article and speculating with the shop owner about the future of indoor lighting.

She kissed him on the cheek and whispered in his ear, "Buy me a peppermint stick, will you?"

He gave her an absent-minded nod, so she turned to Jess in irritation. "Honey, would you mind?" She hooked her arm through his and led him outside.

He did mind. While not as interested in streetlights as the others, Jess was keen to learn the latest local news and with that suss out their job prospects. He escorted her to the bank anyway, thinking that the sooner they could put her on that train the better. He knew Adam had been hatching a crazy plan to follow her out to Topeka someday, but Jess also knew that Adam would come to his senses when they were rid of her. He always did.

When they cued up behind the only other customer the cashier called out to them from behind the bars, "You're lucky you got here when you did! I'm closing up right after you two."

Jess had never been inside a real bank, and it was smaller than he expected. It consisted of little more than three narrow windows cut out of a floor to ceiling wooden partition that was lined with iron bars. A small opening at the bottom of the middle bars allowed for the passthrough of transactions, but the cynic in Jess noted that the bars weren't very close together anyway. He wondered if they weren't just for show.

When Betty asked if he was working hard all by himself, the friendly cashier confirmed her suspicion and overshared that his daughter's new husband had once agreed to work for him but was instead trying his hand at prospecting. He made a sad face and muttered something about the deadly gold fever.

Jess was alarmed by Betty's line of questioning, but

the cashier didn't seem to mind her intrusive nature and seemed flattered, if slightly uncomfortable, when she exclaimed that he couldn't possibly be old enough to have a married daughter.

Jess rolled his eyes and stepped to the side when it was her turn in line. He figured that her finances—or lack thereof—were none of his business.

"Here's what I need." She made a show of hiding the paper with her arm as she wrote a note and then smiled sweetly while slipping it under the bars.

The cashier's eyes widened as he read it and Jess had barely enough time to register the jolt of warning that shot down his spine before he spotted Betty poking that little pistol of hers between the bars.

"God dammit, woman. What are you doing?" He moved to grab her, but she turned the gun on him.

"I'm getting out of here. For good," she said, and again aimed at the cashier. "Hurry up, honey."

Jess's fingers twitched over the pistol on his hip as the cashier reached under the counter. His eyes darted from Betty to the man and while he contemplated where one could shoot a woman without killing her, the cashier pushed a small bag of coins under the bars.

Betty snatched up the bag and shook it at him, keeping her pistol aimed at his head. "I wrote that I wanted the paper—"

Before she could finish her sentence, the cashier brought his other hand from under the counter and brandished a pistol of his own.

Jess drew his gun, hollering, "Everybody just calm the fuck down!"

"Give me the paper!" Betty snapped at the cashier and then muttered to herself, "Why don't men ever listen?"

The cashier swung his pistol from Betty to Jess and cocked the hammer.

"Don't do this," Jess pleaded with him. "She's just crazy, nobody has to get hurt."

She narrowed her eyes and said, "Don't call me crazy." Shooting through the bars, she grazed the cashier in the shoulder. He didn't have it in him to shoot a lady, so he turned on Jess and fired. It all happened so fast that Jess would have a hard time believing it happened at all if it weren't for the bullet hole under his ribcage.

As the cashier fell against the counter, Betty grabbed his pistol and shot him. Knowing how it would look to the town, she took full advantage. Thinking Jess was dead, or at least dying, she would blame him for everything and still get on the train–perhaps with Adam in tow.

From next door, Adam heard the shots and when he burst into the bank, Betty was screaming, "Help! Someone!" while stuffing the coins into her petticoat pockets and reaching through the bars for the drawer of bills behind the counter.

"Shut up, Betty." Adam growled and knelt beside Jess on the wooden floor.

"She stole the money," Jess rasped. "I think she killed him...and I think he killed me."

"Easy, easy. You're gonna be fine." Adam tried to soothe him, but tears jumped into his eyes when he pulled open Jess's coat. His white shirt was nearly soaked with red and each ragged breath he took seemed to require so much of his strength that Adam feared his friend was already using up his reserves.

A few people began to gather at the door, and someone ran for the sheriff.

"We've got to go." Ignoring his pained groans, Adam hauled Jess up and steadied him with an arm around his waist. Jess leaned heavily against him, barely able to walk, but Adam drew his pistol to get them past the small, confused crowd. He worked furiously to get them mounted on his horse, keeping alert for the sheriff. As he got Jess situated in front of him, he felt Betty pull on his leg.

"You're leaving me?" She cried, backing away from the advancing crowd. "Where am I supposed to go now?"

"Bitch," his hands, covered in Jess's blood, shook as he held the pistol to her forehead, "you can go to hell."

Adam dug his heels into the sides of his horse hoping Jess would survive the rough ride ahead. He knew there would be a posse hunting them down in a matter of hours, but Jess was fading fast, and they made it only as far as the Hinojosa ranch.

They'd been friendly with the family in the past and though Adam hated to put them in such a position, they were more than happy to help. Even so, if Jess recovered at all, it would take a long time and the patriarch had to tell Adam that he couldn't hide them both.

Clemente Hinojosa had friends everywhere it seemed, and he told Adam of a mining camp called Cottonwood. It was out of a posse's reach but not so far that they couldn't get word to him of Jess's condition. It was a rough place, but he was sure Adam would find it easy to fit in.

Adam rode out the next morning. Angry, lonely and desperately afraid for his brother.

Chapter Twenty-Seven

"I had to lay low," Adam told Bash, "and, there's no place lower than the mines."

"But, he lived, right?" Though they'd never met, Bash felt an odd affinity for Jess.

"Yep." Adam smiled. "He was one tough son of a gun. We were wanted up north for bank robbery and murder and if they caught us together, they'd hang us. It was a few years before I would see him again." Sadness crossed Adam's face as he remembered those dark times, but his eyes lit up again as he remembered the more cheerful days that followed.

"By then Jess had met Cory and he'd become a lawman *of sorts*. I rode with them for a while and then I went to Bisbee. We made sure that we were never separated for that long again though, and he was there for me when I needed him most."

Bash found that he liked Jess as much as he hated Betty, and he hoped Adam never stopped telling stories about their adventures together; but the sun was coming up and if they were going to live to tell their own stories, they would have to rest. The others spread their blankets and sleeping bags on the floor with the dogs curled up around their legs, but he and Laura had managed to commandeer the couch. She was seated upright, nestled against the pillows in the corner, and he laid his head in her lap.

It had been his intention to grab a cat nap and then make some plans, but he was exhausted, and slept hard as she ran her fingers through his hair. Michael had turned him completely gray during their last battle as Heaven's Watch, and Bash had struggled to adjust; but Laura found it softened the edges of her tough sheriff and she couldn't keep her hands out of it.

She struggled for a while but finally gave up on the idea of sleep. The wind had died down outside, and the glow of the firelight was warm as it danced around her friends. She took comfort in the sight of them scattered in restless sleep throughout the room.

Except for Sam. It wasn't the man himself who made her nervous, but what he'd seen, and what he'd done; and because of her own past, not to mention what she was sure to do in the future, she couldn't judge him for any of it.

She brushed a strand of hair away from Sebastian's eyes and realized that she'd placed an unfair burden on Sam. Every one of her friends had done bad things for what they hoped were good reasons. Good enough, anyway. There was no shame in wondering if they would all meet again in Hell.

Scanning the room, she caught Adam staring at her and gave him a reassuring smile. He'd finished off another beer, but it didn't appear to her that it had achieved the desired effect. The sun was rising, and sleep would take him soon, but not before his darkest thoughts had their way with him.

"I know you don't want me here," she whispered, "but I won't let you down."

"Let me down?" He was astonished by what she'd already been willing to sacrifice for him. For them. Scooting closer to the couch, he gave her hand a squeeze. "You're right. I don't want you here, I need you here." He thought again of Cara and added, "No matter how much I wish that wasn't true."

Something occurred to her, and she asked him, "What do you really want, Adam?"

He stared at her.

"Why did you come back to Chuparosa?"

He breathed a heavy sigh. "Cara asked me that once, and it's pretty simple. Some of my happiest years were spent there."

"With Jess and Cory?"

He nodded. "Even as a vampire, I was accepted and loved by my friends in town. We worked side by side until..." his eyes reddened, "until we couldn't anymore."

"It was risky coming back," she said, "but you found the same thing twice. You know that, right?"

"I do." He squeezed her hand again. "Maybe I've lived long enough to come full circle and this time I was lucky enough to find Cara."

Laura's eyes darkened. "Adam, what if..."

"It doesn't matter what she's done, hell if I can somehow avoid it, I don't even want to know. I just want her back."

He stretched out on the floor, pulling the blanket around him. For the briefest of moments, he allowed himself to imagine Cara's homecoming rather than dwell on her absence. Sleep took him so quickly that Laura was jealous. She had her own feelings about Cara's actions to sort out, but that would come later. She rested her head against the back of the couch and at sundown would wake surprised that sleep had come for her too, as soon as she closed her eyes.

Four pistols cocked in unison when about an hour before sunset someone pounded on the door. It was three fist-heavy knocks followed by three more that echoed through the cabin raising the hair on the backs of everyone's necks.

Bash lurched up from the couch and put one hand on the doorknob as Sam and Doug kicked away the blankets and took up positions in two corners of the cramped room. Adam stood next to Bash on the other side of the hinges with his fangs lowered, and Laura scooped some flames from the fireplace into her palm while ushering Angie to the kitchen. Bash gave the others a nod and then threw open the door.

"Jesus Christ!" A frazzled and freezing Seth held up his hands.

Bash blew out the breath he'd been holding and lowered his gun. "Get in here," he ordered as Seth began to hop from foot to foot in the cold.

After some brief introductions for Doug's and Angie's benefit, Seth started unpacking his olive-green messenger bag at the kitchen table. Clumps of mud and pine needles fell from tangled cords as he sorted out the equipment.

"It's a good thing you're so paranoid because the bad guys are, in fact, out to get you," he said, plugging a small tablet into a portable power block. After a few taps on the screen, he motioned for them to gather around as the playback from his trail camera started up.

"Walter took off with one of his goons, but they'll be back because they left two women in the shack."

Certain that one of them was Cara, Adam exchanged a worried look with Laura.

"They also have a prisoner," Seth continued, replaying the section of video where the lavender haired vampire lugged him inside.

"Who *is* she?" Sam squinted at the screen, but the blowing snow and the distance made it impossible to see her face.

"No clue," Seth admitted. "The hostage is not a vampire–not yet anyway. But you can bet he's running out of blood so our sense of urgency just increased times ten."

At one point what looked like a fur covered rope whipped in front of the camera, but it was gone as quickly as it appeared.

"Wait," Bash leaned in for a closer look, "what was that?"

"What was what?" Seth quickly put the camera back on its 'live' setting.

"Was it a cable or something? You must have seen it," Bash insisted, looking to the others for validation. They hadn't noticed, so he let it go, but he mentally filed away Seth's obvious relief.

"Will you please focus?" Seth laid out photographs of the shack. "Right now, there's one vampire posted in front and two in back." He pointed out that the hunter's shack sat near the rim of a shallow canyon. "Take advantage of this ledge and Walter's absence–split up and come at them from each side. You are definitely riding into a trap, but Cara's still a wildcard. If you kill the guards and storm the inside, you might be able to turn the tables and get the jump on Walter when he gets back."

Sam sighed and leaned back in his chair. "If and might are not exactly my favorite words."

"All hell is sure to break loose," Seth conceded, "but Walter lured you up here for a reason." He turned his attention to Adam. "He needs you for something, and that's our real advantage."

The worst part of the storm had been the wind, knocking out the power and the already tenuous cell service, but the weather had calmed significantly while they'd slept through the day.

The evening was so clear that what snow remained sparkled in the moonlight as Bash stared through the shutter slats in the kitchen. The cold weather amped up the ever-present dull ache in his bones and he groaned as he raised his arms overhead for a full body stretch. He turned to hoist his bag onto his shoulder to find Doug reaching out to him with a bottle of ibuprofen in his hand.

"Lifesaver." Bash accepted the medicine with a grateful smile and dosed out two pills, paused, then dropped one more in his palm before swallowing them with the last of his coffee.

"Alright," Seth announced after doing final checks on their radios, "Doug and Angie will stay here and monitor our movements. Adam and Bash will come in from the front on the horses while I take Sam, Laura, and the dogs by the low road. They'll make the short climb up that shallow ridge, attacking from behind. I'll wait there as backup for whoever is left."

Doug hoped that last part was unnecessarily ominous. "I wish there was more I could do," he said.

"You are mission critical," Seth reminded him. "I need you to keep your eyes on that camera feed and let us know if things go sideways. And if we all end up dead, call one of those numbers I gave you. There's a very particular emergency medical service for that sort of cleanup."

"No pressure." Sam laughed and slapped Doug on the back.

Angie reached up to give Laura a hug and when she did, the thick silver necklace she wore pulled out from under her collar and fell across her chest. Adam blanched and used his hand to cover his face as the candlelight cast the metal's reflection in his eyes.

"Oh, sorry." Angie moved to tuck it back in, but he gave her a dismissive wave.

"We're allergic," he said, "so, you might as well keep it out, just in case."

"Allergic?" Sam was incredulous. "How bad of a reaction are we talking about?"

"It will poison my blood if it gets on me," Adam explained. "How's that for a reaction?"

"Why didn't you tell us about this *allergy* on the boat?"

"Because I didn't want you using it on me. Besides, for someone who hunts monsters for a living, you sure don't know much about them."

"It might shock you to learn that little gems like that are damn hard to come by. You're the only vampire who's been kind enough to share his life story with me."

"Thank you for reminding me, Angie." Adam took the hat pin cylinder from his duffel bag and handed it to Laura.

She turned it over in her hands, careful to keep it from catching the light. "It's beautiful."

"Use it if you need to and keep it if you don't," he instructed. "It's yours now."

Her hair hung in a loose ponytail that stuck out of the adjustable band of her Diamondbacks baseball cap. It was not the best tactical arrangement, but it kept her curls out of her face. Adam's hat pin gave her an idea. She twisted the curls into a bun secured with a wide elastic and then pushed the pin through the band until all that showed was the turquoise bead at the top.

"Let's get moving." Seth led Adam and Bash, followed closely by a suspicious Carl, outside to his Ranger and tossed them each an apple from the back.

The crunch of their boots was the only sound they heard until the horses sensed them rounding the corner. Saddled and waiting, two untethered chestnut quarter horses snorted and dragged their hooves through the mud, seemingly anxious to get going.

Adam offered his apple to the closest one. "You just left them out here?" He asked.

"These horses are just fine," Seth assured him.

While she snacked on his apple, Bash ran his hand along the other horse's shoulder. Seth appeared to be right. Too right. He'd felt an instant connection to his horse, Tess, in the Sheriff's stable back home, but it was nothing like the warm acceptance he was receiving from the animal in front of him just then.

"How did you get them here?" Bash wondered,

noting the absence of a trailer.

"Listen Columbo," Seth snapped, "my job is logistics so why don't you just let me logist?"

Bash had no intention of doing that, but they were interrupted by Laura, who'd come out to see him off.

Her breath caught in her throat at the sight of him, tall and rugged in his sherpa lined coat. She buried her fingers in the soft the collar and pressed her hips to his. "My god, you are a handsome man."

Even in the darkness she could see him blush. He touched his forehead to hers and then gave her a long slow kiss.

"If anything happens to me," he started.

"It won't."

"Dammit woman..." It was not the time for stubbornness, and she had to face the facts that their odds of survival weren't great—or even good for that matter.

Looking into his eyes, she spoke as if she were giving him nuclear codes to memorize. "It's. Not. Our. Time."

Unsure if he wanted to know the answer, he braced himself and asked, "How do you know that?"

"It's a feeling I've had for a while." She patted the horse's neck. "It certainly won't be easy, but this fight isn't about us, and it's not going to take us."

"I don't know baby," he ran a hand through his hair, "it sure feels pretty close to home."

She affixed his cowboy hat on his head. "I can't say exactly why, and I don't know how it *will* happen, but we're not going to die up here."

He was so stunned by how certain she seemed that he couldn't' help but trust her, and he felt his fears abating. Somewhat.

Seth and Adam kept busy during that intimate exchange by convincing an unwilling Carl to stay behind.

Carl wanted to go with Adam and the *big man*, but he reluctantly moved to Laura's side.

"You're a good boy." Adam knelt and snuggled with his dog. "Help Watson take care of her."

After they saddled up, Bash squeezed Laura's hand, and she was grateful that they rode off before her tears had a chance to fall. Carl looked up, sensing her rising stress level and nudged his nose against her knees. She gave his ears a scratch and said, "We're not going to die, Carl, but we're in for one hell of a fight."

Chapter Twenty-Eight

Back inside, Laura took a vial of peppermint essential oil from her pouch and dabbed some behind her ears before handing it to Sam. "They're also allergic to this." It was a detail she'd learned when her niece once tried to burn a peppermint wand in Adam's presence, nearly closing off his windpipe.

Sam rubbed the liquid between his hands, aware of how hers were beginning to shake. The pent-up energy from the spell casting, worry for Bash, and fear for herself was overwhelming Laura's nervous system. Keeping it together for everyone was beginning to take its toll on her body and she began to feel particularly prickly.

She was riding a wave of hormones that tossed her between the urges to crumble, sobbing in the corner and to pick up the nearest heavy thing and use it to beat Sam to death. At that moment she irrationally blamed him for everything that had ever gone wrong in her life.

To his credit, Sam recognized the beads of perspiration on her forehead and the shift in her demeanor, and scooped some ice from the cooler into a dishtowel.

As her vision tunneled, Laura fought with the zipper on her hoodie. She finally shrugged out of it as her body temperature soared, soaking her t-shirt in sweat. Her skin crawled with the all too familiar feeling of being burned alive from the inside by the hot flash.

"Here, honey." Angie took the ice pack and pressed it to the back of Laura's neck as Sam eased her down on the couch.

He touched her cheek and smoothed the flyaway hair away from her flushed skin. "Aren't you half angel? Don't you get a pass from all this?"

Laura frowned. "I'm afraid that's not how it works."

"Heinous bullshit," he said, adding quietly after a moment, "My mother killed herself during menopause."

"Good god, Sam." Laura sat up straight, but too quickly, and fell back from dizziness. "I'm so sorry," she said, and moved the ice to her forehead.

"It's a lonely time for a woman," his voice took on an acid tone as he added, "and it ain't fair."

Doug and Seth looked up from the kitchen table to report that Bash and Adam had reached the first marker. "We need to go."

Laura had nearly wilted while putting on her coat and gloves but was already freezing again as she climbed into the Ranger next to Seth. She waved to Angie as the dogs jumped in the back with Sam.

Fascinated and afraid, Angie leaned into Doug, who gave her a tight squeeze before returning to the monitor and radio. She sat beside him scratching furiously in a notebook with a pencil.

Without looking away from the monitor he asked, "Are you writing about all of this?"

Her new friends were the bravest people she'd ever met, and she was determined to document their story, even if only for those who were left behind.

"You bet your ass I am."

The group was travelling light, but deadly. They didn't expect to use their guns on anyone but themselves, should things go completely off the rails. No offense to Adam, but not one of his friends was willing to become a vampire.

Sam carried a compact crossbow with bolts he'd carved himself from thick juniper branches, Bash's machete was strapped to his side and the pouch on Laura's hip was loaded with dark magic. Adam's body was his weapon, and the closer they got to the hunter's shack, the more charged up he felt.

"Whoa." he motioned to Bash and tightened his knees against the saddle. Their horses slowed with only the lightest grip on the reins. They'd instantly melded their trots to their riders and though the temperature was freezing, the men were kept warm by a gentle heat that emanated from their hides.

They came to a standstill on the edge of a clearing and Adam leaned over to stroke his horse's neck. He gave voice to the question they'd both had since leaving Chuck's cabin. "Where do you suppose Seth came across these spectacular animals?"

"I've always known that there's more to Seth than he lets on, but I assumed his ability to get weird things was related to some sort of criminal history. Sam's department isn't that particular when it comes to the selection process," Bash chuckled, "but I'm beginning to think Seth's connections are more mystical than illegal."

Adam nodded. "Speaking of mystical," he turned in the saddle to gaze at the mountains looming craggy and deep purple in the darkness. "People thought I was crazy to stay in Arizona. It wasn't just the sun—to this day it can be a dangerous place. But really, how could I have lived anywhere else?"

Though Bash was a little unnerved by Adam's slip into the past tense, he said only, "In my experience the most dangerous places attract the bravest people."

He radioed their position and Doug confirmed that Laura and Sam were on their way. "Ready?"

Adam gave Bash's short but loaded question a sharp nod and they both hollered, "Hyah!"

As the horses took off through the meadow at full gallop, Adam's wistfulness was replaced with icy resolve. Until then he'd been loath to contemplate the possibilities, focusing instead on their battle plan; but win or lose, he knew that his life was about to change forever.

* * *

Rance's blood had a sweetness that Cara couldn't put her finger on. He tasted nothing like that of the criminals she'd devoured in the past and her strength began to return with the first swallow. Still, even if she drained him to the point of death it still wouldn't be enough for a full recovery. As her vision cleared, she noticed with horror how young he was and weighed her mind-numbing thirst against her desire to keep him safe. *Just a little more, Rance...good boy.*

Soon, his body convulsed against hers and though the result was what felt like a laser searing through her brain, she forced herself to pull away.

"Did you get enough?" He croaked.

"We're about to find out."

Betty came out of the bedroom, flung open the back door and barked a few orders at the guards. When their responses were lacking, she marched outside shouting something about how she was in charge when Walter was gone. Rance could tell from the conversation that, out of curiosity, the front guard had joined the others around back.

He made a snap decision, accurately calculating how quickly he could make it out the front door, but not considering how weak his body would be from the loss of blood. He might have made it, but as dizziness overtook him, he fell against a flimsy wooden end table, toppling it with the noise equivalent of a car crash.

"Hey!" Betty was across the room in under a second and Cara winced at the sickening crunch his shattering bones made as she stomped on his ankle.

Rance cried out and pulled his knees to his chest in a weak attempt to get away from her, but she lifted him by the collar and tossed him against the wall next to Cara who remained as still as possible.

"Don't try that shit again," Betty snapped.

She jerked Cara's head up by the hair to make sure she was still alive and then let it fall back down with a thud. Cara searched the beautiful blue eyes of Adam's former lover for some sign of leftover humanity but found none. Even after she'd been captured, Cara had wavered in her judgment of Betty. Walter wandered the earth unchecked, doling out evil on the defenseless. He was exactly the kind of monster she hunted, and Betty might have once been the kind of woman she tried to protect from him, but that was no longer the case.

She thought of the kids at the warehouse, the couple in Phoenix, the tortured witches, and the incalculable others, at last resolving to kill the woman she'd once wanted so badly to befriend. Rance was trying to be brave but as she watched him writhing in pain, Cara knew that she wasn't just going to kill Betty, she was going to rip her to pieces.

Chapter Twenty-Nine

"I'll be right here when you get back," Seth assured Laura and Sam. His optimism was appreciated, if not shared.

As they made their way up the ravine, Watson and Carl ran ahead, periodically turning to monitor their progress. The dogs noted with some agitation that after each switchback, the man trailed farther and farther behind their Laura.

"Hold up!" Sam called out as quietly as he could and leaned against a large boulder to catch his breath. When she backtracked to meet him, he wheezed, "You're one of those cardio bunnies, aren't you?"

She rolled her eyes. "Chuparosa is surrounded by mountains, Sam. I've been hiking my entire life."

A random thought had occurred to him while he'd been trying to avoid Hypoxia, and he was curious about her take on it.

"Adam treats being a vampire like it's some kind of murderous chronic condition," he said, "but if there were a cure, do you think he'd take it?"

She pondered his question for a minute. Adam hated drinking blood for survival, but he was happy to flex his supernatural strength, whether he was lending a hand to Heaven's Watch or pulling apart a goblin-one of his favorite activities. He'd enjoyed his long life, but the loss of his loved ones along the way had taken a massive toll so, in the end, Laura wasn't comfortable answering for him.

She answered for herself instead. "I hope he doesn't, but I'm selfish and I don't want to lose any of my friends."

"Does that include me," he gave her an uncharacteristically sheepish grin, "or am I forever on your shit list?"

She thought for another long moment. "It didn't include you, but I think now it might."

The shack taken over by the vampires sat near the edge of a plateau overlooking a partially frozen creek that snaked through a narrow valley below. Adam and Bash hitched their horses less than a quarter mile away just as Sam and Laura cleared the ridge.

The dogs circled anxiously but obeyed Laura's command to stay quiet, even though Carl had caught Adam's scent. The Pit bull's instinct to bound away and greet him was eclipsed by his need to make Adam proud by protecting the woman.

Bash's jaw tightened as he raised his binoculars and through the window saw Cara chained to the wall. He nudged Adam, putting a finger to his lips as he handed him the binoculars.

The fury Adam had kept locked up inside for days

suddenly burst free at the sight of the purple-haired vampire standing over his lover's broken body. Heat radiated from under his collar as he crushed the binoculars in his angry hands, but then a chill settled deep in his bones as she turned to face the window.

"Oh, my god," he breathed, "it's Betty."

"Betty?" Bash pulled Adam into the trees. "Your Betty? *The* Betty?"

A clump of snow fell around them as Adam punched the trunk of a Douglas Fir. "Did she find Walter in Bisbee after I was turned? Did he go after her?" He was torturing himself. "Christ, Bash it's been over a hundred years. How could I not have known?"

"I bet she lured Cara out to get to you." Bash reasoned.

Adam looked up at him. "Sebastian, Betty hates me. If she's working with Walter..."

Bash put one hand on Adam's shoulder and with the other raised the radio. Speaking low, he said, "We've got eyes on Cara. She's hurt and she's in the house but head's up everyone: so is Betty."

"*The* Betty?" Sam asked. "She's a vampire?"

"Yes, god dammit. So things just got much worse."

Back at Chuck's cabin, Angie squeezed Doug's hand. His shoulders were glued to his ears, but he managed to keep his voice calm as he reported, "They all look to be vampires, but I still only see three guards. Is there anyone else in the house?"

"There's a guy on the floor next to Cara," Adam said, "Looks like he might be the new prisoner, but keep an eye out for him. And let us know the second you see Walter."

Laura scanned the house with her own binoculars,

narrowing her eyes as she followed Betty's erratic movements. She tore open a bag of chips, knelt to wave it in front of the boy and then stood, popping one in her mouth with a giggle. But for the hair color she was just as Adam described and Laura hated her. Most women had reasons for the sketchy shit they did—good ones too—but Betty was cruel for the sake of it.

In Laura's mind Betty was a woman not content to have it all without also making sure that others had nothing. She wondered if life with a man like Walter was worth the payoff, which from where Laura stood was not that large.

Adam couldn't afford to worry about his ex if he had to fight Walter, and Bash and Sam would have their hands full. She reached out and Watson pressed himself to her side, conveying that somehow, he knew what she was thinking.

"I see her," Laura told the others, "and she's mine."

She eyed one of the guards, dug in her pouch for the poisoned patches and turned to Sam. "I'm about to create one hell of a diversion."

He pulled the crossbow from its sling and said, "I got your back, A-Team."

One of the guards, apparently tasked by Betty with gathering wood, began breaking fallen branches over his knee and tossing the logs against the shack. The other guard snickered, taunting, "Mom will snap if those are too wet."

The first guard flipped him off and pushed through the trees where Laura waited. He crunched his boot on a rotting log, and she had to cover her mouth to hold back a scream as dozens of insects scurried across her boots. The vampire kicked away the bigger beetles but as he bent over to flick a stubborn centipede from the cuff of his jeans, Laura reached through the branches and stuck one of her patches to his neck.

"Hey!" He slapped at the patch, thinking it was one of the insects, but forgot about it as he caught sight of Laura disappearing into the brush.

"What do you see?" The other guard was at his side so quickly that it was a jarring reminder for Laura to be wary of their speed.

The first guard became transfixed with the second one as the hallucinogenic drugs filtered through his senses. He stared doltish and slack jawed as, before his eyes, the second vampire morphed into the kind of man he'd always wanted to be before Walter had turned him into a vampire against his will. The kind of man that represented everything he'd lost, the kind of man that he now hated the most. A hero. A fireman.

He took a few steps toward the second guard, mistaking his mustard-colored barn coat for turnout gear. He grabbed him by the collar and shoved him against the wall.

"What is your problem?"

Flanked by the dogs, Sam and Laura moved through the shadows, approaching with caution as the first guard pushed the second one's head to the side and lowered his fangs. It was too late by the time the second guard realized what was happening and he emitted a gurgling scream as his punctured vein began to gush.

Since vampires cannot safely drink from each other, the attacker was overcome with more pain and confusion with each swallow as the blood he sucked from his companion seared the lining of his throat. He tore his mouth away, doubling over and staggering to the porch from where he spotted Laura. She looked to him like a horrible, clawed creature he'd once seen in a late-night movie, and he shrank away as she moved in his direction. His vision flickered then, and she was once again just a woman in the woods.

"Bitch!"

Though his organs were failing, he advanced on her, but was taken down by Watson and Carl. He screamed as the dogs tore at his body, appearing to his drug addled mind as the creatures he'd feared most as a child. Werewolves.

Sam whistled for the dogs to get out of the way and raised his crossbow, but the second vampire was on him before he could fire, lifting him by the neck and throwing him into the trees.

Laura flicked her phosphorescent fingernail polish and covered him in a blanket of fire. His power of speed was greatly diminished, and he lumbered toward her, giving Sam, who had dislocated his shoulder in the fall, just enough time to aim and shoot. He dropped his head in relief when the bolt punctured the vampire's chest.

He grasped and pulled at what he could reach of the shaft, but the juniper sank deep, and the stench of burning copper wafted over them as blood flowed from the vampire's eyes, nose and mouth. He fell first to his knees and then on his face before dying in a dirt encrusted pile of snow.

The dogs were able to keep the first guard down as Laura helped Sam to his feet, but the power in her patch was wearing off and he batted Carl away. The Pit bull hit the dirt with a yelp but scrambled up quickly, looking to the humans for direction as Watson bit down on the vampire's ribs.

"Get him off me!" he cried, presumably to Betty, who had been watching the entire battle with giddy interest from the kitchen window.

"Watson!" Laura called.

The German Shepherd ran to her as Sam nocked a bolt and fired into the vampire's abdomen. The guard pulled it out and tossed it away, glaring at them as he pushed off the ground. Sam's aim was trash, and his strength was waning, so Laura lit the fresh bolt on fire and with a tiny prayer and an anguished howl, Sam raised the crossbow overhead to fire at the vampire soaring over them.

A mini bonfire erupted from his chest, and he fell to the snow with a guttural scream. He gathered himself up and burst through the back door covered in flames, collapsing just over the threshold. Laura stood out of sight by the door trying not to gag as the skin hanging from the torn away places left by the dogs began to sizzle.

Wincing as he reached for the radio, Sam reported, "Two down."

Chapter Thirty

"What now?" The guard who had returned to the front let out a dramatic groan at the sound of the commotion, but snuffed out his cigarette and meandered around the cabin where he was confronted by Bash, who stepped out of the trees with his gun drawn.

"Freeze!" he shouted.

The guard laughed out loud, cracked his knuckles and dropped his fangs. He had to give the mortal man props for his courage, but he was going to bleed him dry and drop him at Walter's feet like a Christmas present—maybe improving the bastard's mood a little bit. He hadn't seen Adam perched on the roof, and though he lunged for Bash with lightning speed, Adam sprang and tackled them all to the ground before he could sink his fangs.

Bash scrambled out of the way as the vampires faced off and smeared a trickle of blood away from his neck, thinking, *that was damn close.*

The guard towered over Adam and with a considerable amount of bulk to work with, assumed he could make quick work of the smaller man. At close to five foot ten, Adam had been taller than most as a younger man, but over the years he'd seen both men and women eclipse him in height and had learned to use his stature to his advantage when necessary. As they charged at one another, he tucked his head, lowered his shoulder, and turned inward, cracking the guard's ribs with the force of their collision.

He flew backward, crashing into what remained of the woodpile and Adam pounced, straddling him before he even hit the ground. The guard wrapped his hands around Adam's throat, but the harder he pressed his thumbs into Adam's windpipe, the harder Adam squeezed his knees against the sides of his splintered chest.

Finally, the guard hollered out in pain, let go and reached for one of the scattered logs. Adam took it from him and brought it down hard against the side of his head over and over, beating the guard unconscious.

Bash heaved Adam to his feet and unsheathed his machete. "Stand back," he ordered, but it turned out that neither of them was clear of the arterial spray when Bash severed the guard's head from his shoulders. He did it with such practiced speed and precision that Adam shuddered.

"That's another reason I'm glad we're friends," he said.

No longer amused by the fighting, Betty shouted for the front guard, but it was Adam who kicked in the door with Bash close on his heels. Giving Betty barely a glance, Adam ripped Cara's chain ring out of the wall and knelt beside her.

Tears streamed down her dirty, pale face as he lifted her chin. "I fucked up," she sobbed.

"You and me both."

While Sam and the dogs hung back, Laura slipped inside unnoticed and crouched behind the kitchen sink, as close to Betty as she dared.

Completely unmoored by the sight of Adam so lovingly attending to Cara, Betty began to shake with rage.

"You bastard!" She ran at him, but fast as she was, Laura had been expecting her attack and kicked her feet out from underneath her. As she fell, Carl jumped over the dead vampire on the back doorstep and blocked her path, snarling and snapping his jaws.

Laura flicked her fingernails, filled her palms with fire and hovered over Betty.

"It's my understanding that vampires don't like fire any more than witches do," she said.

"Heads up," Doug's voice came over their radios, "Walter is pulling in the drive and he's got two more goons with him."

Betty smirked at Laura and stood up, but Laura noted that she looked worried by Walter's return.

"Adam, he's here," Bash warned, taking his place beside Cara as the Jeep doors slammed out front.

Cara squeezed his arm, "Walter used me...this is a trap."

"We know sweetheart," Bash said, his eyes darting from Adam to the door hanging off its hinges, "he wants Adam."

"He wants Chuparosa."

Bash gaped at her. "What?"

She had no time to explain before Walter sauntered in behind the two vampires Doug had cautioned them about. He pulled down the door and tossed it aside.

"Impressive entrance," Walter said. "I saw what you did to my men. You know how difficult it is to make them and that's going to cost you," he cast a glance at Cara, "but we'll talk about that later."

"What do you want?" Adam asked, his voice was acid.

"An armed escort into our new home."

Walter chuckled at Adam's apparent confusion. "I could never allow only one of us walk away from the fight because you give me something to do when I get bored." He kicked the side table away, clearing a path between them. "You love this modern world, so I guess it was just a matter of time before you found the perfect place for us."

"There's no place for you," Adam growled.

"But there is, and you're going to be my host. I even brought Miss Betty along, providing you with a harem of sorts. I figure I can cobble together one of my own from what Chuparosa has to offer," he said, leering at Laura.

Adam finally faced Betty and tried to keep his voice steady. "You could have told me."

"All this time I thought you were rotting in Hell, but now that the secrets are out," she glared at Walter, "let's not be petty. Take us to your piece of shit town so we can be one big happy family at last."

"You had your chance for that," Adam said.

"You're not still mad that I killed Jess, are you?" Betty tossed her hair and put her hands on her hips. "I did you a favor and you know it. That that stupid cripple was ruining everything."

"Boy are you in for a surprise," Laura murmured.

"You shot him," Adam smiled to himself and shook his head, "but you didn't kill him."

"Liar," Betty whispered.

"We were the best of friends until the end of his long, long life."

Betty's face fell. She'd convinced herself over the years that though Adam had been unwilling to devote himself to her, she'd at least gotten revenge on him by killing Jess.

"Liar!" She screamed.

Walter reached out and backhanded her into silence. "Shut up whore, this is not about you."

Bash took advantage of the commotion to assess the prisoner. Brushing his fingers against the bite marks on the boy's neck, he asked Cara, "Who is this guy?"

"This is Rance," Cara hung her head, "and he saved my life."

Bash sighed eyeing the swollen, bruised up leg. "Can you walk, son?"

"My ankle's broken," Rance kept his voice low, "but I'm not as messed up as I've been playing at."

"Good." Bash reevaluated him with hopefulness. "This is gonna get ugly so stay low."

"It's *gonna* get ugly?"

Bash patted his shoulder and said, "Just keep your eyes on me, and don't do anything crazy."

"Don't worry," Rance sniffed, "I'm leaving the crazy to you guys."

"...but Chuparosa's taken." Laura was saying as Bash took his place at Adam's side.

Betty sidestepped Carl to get to Cara but once again

Laura had been waiting for her to do just that and drew a protective ring of fire around Cara's body. Crazed with fury, she whirled on Laura, who grew the fireball in her hands to the size of a basketball and said, "I dare you."

Cara didn't wait for Betty to test Laura's resolve. She used much of her renewed strength to lurch through the flames and take Betty out at the knees. Betty jumped up and jerked Cara to her feet, throwing her into Laura and snuffing out her fire. The two women tumbled over the dead vampire and out the back door into Sam and Watson.

"That stupid cow has always been more trouble than she's worth," Walter sneered, "and if that witch doesn't kill her, I'm going to do it myself."

Something we can actually agree on, thought Bash, just before Walter ordered his men to attack.

Outside Laura helped Cara to stand while Sam tried to nock another bolt, but Betty took his crossbow and flung it off the ledge into the ravine. She caught his fist as he took a clumsy swing at her and then bit down on his hand, biting her way up his arm until her fangs landed in his brachial artery.

Watson attacked, locking his jaws around her calf until she released Sam's punctured arm with a scream and a spray of blood. The air crackled around them, and Laura called Watson away before firing a stream of electricity into Betty's torso that knocked her to her knees. Laura had been careful with the amount of power she used but Sam still caught some of the jolt and collapsed unconscious.

Betty picked up a stick and crawled around, drawing

symbols in the mud until Cara remembered their conversation about the demon.

"Laura, stop her!" she shouted.

"You know," Sam's blood ran from Betty's lips as she spoke, "if witches didn't have their occasional uses, I would make it my mission in life to burn you all to ash."

She pulled an old leather pouch from her pocket and sprinkled a handful of copper colored dust over the lines while muttering quietly to herself. Soon thin tendrils of smoke rose from the inside of the sigil as she spoke.

"Shit." Laura recognized a summoning when she saw one and she was damn sure that it wasn't an angel Betty was calling up. The earth underneath them began to rumble and shake and an old scent hovered over them as the airy body of what might have once been a giant of a man stepped out of the circle.

Chapter Thirty-One

"Kill her!" Betty shouted.

The space around him filled with electricity that he gathered up and twisted through his fingers, forming a long whip.

"Oh, no," Laura breathed.

The demon cracked the whip and lashed the fall across Laura's back as she dove for the bushes. Collapsing in a pile of snow, she played dead, furious that she'd let him best her so quickly. When her inflamed skin became unbearable, she rolled over in the icy dirt to soothe the pain, only to find him hovering a few feet away.

She threw a thick stream of fire into his enormous body, which was materializing more and more with each passing second, so much so that he was able to catch it and reflect it right back at her. She raised her hands and repelled the fire from her face using Rhonda's shield bracelet, but the flames engulfed her all the same.

In a panic, she backed nearly to the edge of the cliff before realizing with awe that the fire was cold and, rather than searing her skin, it was just dancing around her. *Was he playing some kind of game?*

Knowing that Laura would be busy indefinitely with the demon, Betty turned on Cara. She was unaware that Rance had given her his blood, and though its power was doing little more than keeping her upright, Cara intended to use every last bit of her strength until one of them was dead.

"It's supposed to be my turn!" Betty screamed. "I deserve that life!"

"It sounds to me like you rejected that life a long time ago and now you're just bitter." Cara said, moving in.

"Maybe," Betty inched away, luring her closer and closer to the edge, but I'll get it back. I always do."

It was true that Betty was the most capable survivor she'd ever known and even if Adam failed to kill Walter, Betty would eventually figure out a way to do it herself. What she could not stomach was the thought of her moving to Chuparosa, murdering her friends and infecting their town with her version of a bloodborne virus. A full-blown zombie invasion would be better, in Cara's opinion.

The small earthquake that accompanied the demon's appearance had created a fissure and Sam felt the ground cracking as it slowly spread across the plateau. Watson nudged him to sitting though his whole body protested with pains shooting from every muscle. His mind reeled as he looked around. Cara was rushing at

Betty and Laura appeared to be on fire nearby.

He looked at Watson and said, "What the hell is going on?"

Betty yanked Cara to the ground by the hair and when they fell, there was a deafening crack as the ledge gave way and all three women disappeared in a cloud dirt and snow.

"No!" Sam yelled.

Watson ran to the edge and looked back as if to say, "I have no idea what just happened here."

Sam crawled over to meet him and flicked on his flashlight to learn that they were alive and starting to slowly move around. They'd landed on a lower ledge that was as precariously positioned as the one they fell from. If it gave way, he was pretty sure Laura would survive the short fall, assuming she didn't bash her head against one of the hundreds of rocks lining the wash.

"Holy shit!" Seth shouted into the radio. From his post at the bottom of the ravine, he'd seen the ledge plummet.

"Yeah, we got a big problem here," Sam confirmed. "Seth, can you get to them?"

Seth was already climbing up the cliff wall and alerting Doug to *make the call*.

The landslide snuffed out the flames around Laura, but the demon was still with her. He lifted her to her feet, and she turned her head away in revulsion as he brought his face close to hers. Her hat was gone and the bun in her hair had come loose in the fall. He ran his fingers through the messy curls, sniffing at her neck and her ears.

"Nephilim," he said.

She lifted her chin. "What about it?"

He leaned close again, whispering in her ear, "Lucifer has had his hands on you."

She pushed him away, hissing, "Go back to Hell and tell him I said 'hi'."

The demon made a guttural sound, low and menacing, but sad. "The spirits of the Nephilim are earthbound, my cousin."

Her lip trembled slightly. "I don't believe you."

"You are an abomination—I know you believe that. We are cursed to roam unseen until called upon by man," he glanced at Betty, "or woman."

"No." She shook her head. "You're just a demon, and demons lie."

He took her hand. "Someday you too will join the Earth Shadows."

Laura paled and jerked her hand away, light-headed with thoughts racing. Her last and worst punishment for the crime of being born was to be rejection by both Heaven and Hell? It was so horrible that he had to be lying, but at the same time she knew in her heart that he wasn't.

Her thoughts were interrupted by crazed screams, and she spun around to see Cara grab a fistful of Betty's hair and slam her head against the ledge. What was left of Cara's strength would soon run out, so there was no time to dwell on the new information. The Earth Shadow hadn't seemed that keen on following Betty's orders even before he figured out Laura was a Nephilim and that gave her another idea.

"Are you Betty's prisoner?" she asked him.

"I go where I'm called, lest I lose what's left of my

soul," he explained, "but she is no witch and ignores the details within the laws of summoning. The power of blood and names mean nothing to her."

He's free but he's lonely. Laura seized on his suffering. "Tell me your name."

"So that you can make me your slave?" The spirit laughed in her face. "The vampire's stupidity suits me fine."

Laura took the small knife from her pocket and ran it across her palm. "Then I'll make you a deal instead."

He sniffed at the blood trickling off the knife and cocked his head with interest.

"We work together as a team," she offered, "and you never have to be alone again."

"No binding? No contract?"

"Mutual trust," she promised.

The spirit took the knife from her, slit his own palm and said, "Ephraim."

"Ephraim," she repeated and pressed her hand to his.

"Cousin." He interlocked their fingers, and she felt a deep, unsettling connection at once. She'd either just joined forces with one of her ancestors or made a blood pact with an unspeakable evil, but she would have to worry about that later.

Betty and Cara were within striking distance, but Laura was exhausted. Her powers would be unpredictable, and she was not confident that she wouldn't hit Cara. She rubbed her neck and tried to sort out her options. Of her many aches and pains, the one across her back commanded the most attention.

"Ephraim, could you make that whip out of fire?"

He nodded. "And wind and sand and—"

"Got it." The phosphorescent nail polish was nearly worn away from her broken nails, so she unhooked Sam's taser from her belt, flicked the lighter at the bottom and directed the fire at Ephraim, who spun it into a thick glowing cord that dangled three feet from the end of her hand.

She'd never used a whip before and in her worn-out state, it was almost too heavy for her to wield. Even so, she raised it high overhead and snapped it at Betty. The whip cracked dead center, igniting a thin line along her spine, and catching each layer of her hair in a fiery mane around her face.

Betty screamed and grabbed onto Cara, pulling her so close that Laura feared they would both be overwhelmed by the flames after all. Cara scratched at Betty's blistering skin, pulling it away in chunks until Betty shrimped out from underneath her. She tried to roll out the flames but fell onto her back, incapacitated and gasping for breath.

Laura sat down hard on the unstable ledge, her vision blurring from the hot tears that she'd been holding back. The fire alone wouldn't kill Betty, so she rose to all fours and tried crawling to Cara's side, but her body gave out and she toppled over. There was no more she could do for her friend.

In the firelight, Cara caught the glint of something half buried in the snow and when she looked closer, the glare nearly blinded her. *Silver?* She looked at Betty, burning alive but still wheezing out threats. Cara plucked up the long pin and her suspicion was confirmed as the poisonous metal seeped into her skin. With all of her remaining speed, she stabbed the hatpin into Betty's jugular vein hoping she hadn't killed herself in the process.

Betty's body began to twitch, and she gurgled out a white foam as the poison spread through her bloodstream. On the surface of what skin remained, all of her veins became a visible blue, pulsing and seeping out rivulets of toxin. Her infected skin quickly dried and fell from her smoldering bones, but Cara made sure that the last thing Betty saw as she withered away was her smile.

She laid down next to Laura and felt for the rise and fall of her chest. Satisfied that she was still alive, Cara closed her eyes. Weak to the point of hallucinating, she could have sworn she saw Betty's demon stroking Laura's hair.

Chapter Thirty-Two

"Who do you think you are?" One of Walter's new guards eyed Bash up and down with amusement.

"I'm his security," Bash said, nodding in Adam's direction.

"Funny guy." The guard chuckled until Bash drew his pistol and fired three shots into his chest. The vampire was on him so quickly that Bash never saw his hands, he only felt himself flying after the force of the shove and then blunt resistance as he hit the back wall of the shack's tiny bedroom.

The spots in front of his eyes cleared long enough for him to see the guard hovering over him. He squeezed the bullets out of his chest and let them fall on the floor between Bash's legs. Bash supposed the guard must have been a *very* old acquaintance of Walter's to be able to pull that off and was beginning to rethink his strategy.

His cowboy hat had fallen on the floor beside him and to buy himself some time, he made a show of reaching out to put it back on, but the guard flicked it away and jerked him up by the collar.

"Okay, just do it," Bash said, a little disappointed in his choice of last words.

A loud whistle came from the front room and the vampire threw him on the bed and left him there. The frame broke apart from the force of the toss and Bash was grateful for the thin grubby mattress underneath him, amazed that every one of his fifty-two-year-old bones hadn't shattered.

The guards were ordered to start the Jeep, but Adam picked up the front door and swung it to stop Walter from following them out.

Walter punched his fist through the wood, sending shards flying so far that they landed on Bash, who still struggled to lift himself up from the smashed bedframe.

"You're not going to Chuparosa," Adam snarled, "so let's end this right now."

"This ends when and where I say it ends."

The black Jeep pulled up to the porch and Walter dove in the back seat, but Adam jumped on the hood as they tried to get away. He held on through as sharp a donut as a Jeep could manage, but his grip failed as the driver slammed on the brakes. Flung face down in the snow, Adam swore and punched the icy ground. He briefly considered trying to catch them on one of the horses but then Seth called for help over the radio, and he ran around back where he found Bash leaning precariously over a cliff.

"No, no, no," Bash muttered to himself, looking back and forth from Seth who was busily assessing the situation below to Laura who lay motionless in the dirt.

Seth called up, "Bash, she's alive!" He checked Cara's wrist for a pulse and held his fingers there for several seconds before moving them to her neck.

The world around Adam seemed to dissolve and he could hear nothing but the thumping of his heart until the radio crackled. He realized that he hadn't been breathing and took in several gulps of air as Seth reported, "I've got two—repeat two—survivors down here. Our unit's medevac is on the way. Standby to catch this rope."

"Copy that," Bash said, and exchanged looks with Adam before asking Seth, "What about the other one?"

"Nothing but ashes and bone," Seth confirmed.

Bash caught the end of the rope and gave it to Adam. "You okay?"

"I will be."

The chill in Adam's tone made him wonder what exactly was in store for Walter. The punishment would be severe, and Bash intended to help him dole it out, but their priority was getting Laura and Cara safely home.

Adam wrapped the rope around his waist and walked backward, using his strength to pull while Seth and Bash guided the women one by one up the side.

When she reached the top, Laura buried her head in Bash's chest and sobbed.

"It's okay, baby," he rocked her in his arms, "I'm here...I'm here."

Adam wanted nothing more than to hold Cara, but he was glad that she remained unconscious. He hadn't had enough time to sort his feelings for her from his anger with Betty, his worry for his friends and his hatred of Walter. He leaned close to ear and said, "Please know that I love you."

"Don't worry about me guys," Seth hauled himself over the side with a huff. "I'm good."

He waved his arms overhead as the helicopter made a pass with its searchlight and then he counted his team members. "Missing a couple, aren't we Bash?"

"The kid is inside, and..." Bash looked around. "Oh shit."

Even Adam would not have heard Sam's call over the thump of the rotor blades if Watson's ferocious barking hadn't gotten their attention.

"I'm not as fine as the ladies, but could someone help me out over here?"

Knowing he was losing a lot of blood, Sam held up a warning hand as Adam approached. "I don't want to be a vampire," he rasped.

"That's good because I don't want to make you one." Adam ripped the blood-soaked sleeve away from Sam's arm and noticed the odd position of his shoulder.

"This will hurt," he said, and before Sam could protest, he yanked his arm straight to reset the joint.

Sam let out a wail he was grateful the others couldn't hear with all the helicopter noise, but Adam gave him a look that said he was never going to let him forget it.

The medevac landed in a clearing nearby and as they waited for the paramedics, Ephraim appeared next to Laura.

"Jesus Christ!" Bash moved between them. "What the hell is that?"

"That is a very long story," she said. "Ephraim, will you find my sister? Tell her we're alive and give her this." Laura handed him the bloody hatpin wrapped in a handkerchief. "I will see you soon."

"As you wish cousin." A thin whirlwind of dirt and pine needles engulfed the spirit until he disappeared in the dust. When he was gone, the debris fell to the ground.

"We have no idea where Walter's headed," Sam said when the group was gathered.

"I know where he's going." Adam sat next to Cara and held her hand.

"Chuparosa?" Bash wondered.

"Nope. He's going to Bisbee to set another trap."

Bash took off his hat and ran a hand through his hair. "Well, these days, if it's not a trap, then I don't know how to prepare."

Sam said, "That's a five-hour drive and he's got a big head start."

"Wait a minute." Seth smacked his head. "We're not gonna talk about *Ephraim?*" He was met with exasperated stares. "Okay, fine. Well, I can get you to Bisbee in about forty minutes."

They gaped at him.

He patted his chest. "Logistics." The paramedics ran up before he could elaborate and as they loaded Cara on a stretcher, he reminded them about Rance waiting inside the shack.

Laura turned to Bash. "If he can get us there that quickly, we have a chance to wreck Walter's plans."

Bash shook his head. "You're going with the medics."

"I'm going with you." She took an elastic from her pocket and pulled her hair into as tight a ponytail as the pain in her arms would allow.

"You did good, A-Team," Sam said as the medic wrapping his arm eased him onto the stretcher, "damn good, and your job is done. For now."

Laura looked down and stuck a finger in the hole at the knee of her pants. Her bruised and burned body was exhausted, but she could not make herself leave him. He swept her up and laid her on the stretcher and the perceptive paramedic strapped her down before she could rebel. Bash forced a smile, kissed her parched lips and said, "I'll see you tomorrow—I promise."

"She'll be safe with me." Sam gave him a reassuring look and suppressed a pained wince to raise his arm for affect. "Hand to God, or...whoever."

Watson gave Bash's knees a little nudge and then followed the others, jumping into the helicopter as it lifted off. The dog stood at the doorway maintaining eye contact with Bash until they cleared the treetops.

Chapter Thirty-Three

"Have you lost your fucking mind?" Adam hadn't known such loyalty since Jess and once again found himself in the emotional tug of war between deep appreciation and fear for his friend's life.

Bash gave Carl's dirty coat a brush with his hand, repositioned his hat and hoisted his pack onto his shoulder. "Nope," he said, and then turned to ask Seth, "Which way?"

Seth put a finger to his lips to shush them and whistled low. Soon a three-foot tall jackrabbit bounded from around a moss-covered boulder. The rabbit lived on the Other Side of the veil and Bash had seen him before, though he wasn't sure he'd ever get used to him. Seth gave the rabbit a nod and they followed his impatient lead down to the creek at the bottom of the ravine.

The creek was frozen over with a thin crust of ice which the rabbit stomped through with his long foot, motioning for them to do the same. Adam added pneumonia to his worries for Bash as the freezing water soaked through their boots, but they shivered along, following the rabbit midway across the creek. When they'd waded about knee deep, the water warmed and the ice began to flake off the surface, whipping around them in a blinding flurry of crystals.

The current was swift, and they couldn't really see, but Seth urged them to keep going. The water never went over the dog's head, but Adam kept Carl as close as possible until they reached the far bank. The weather had calmed by then and the forest had grown so quiet that their sloshing around seemed deafening. The starlight shone like diamonds off the snow-covered pines and Bash knew at once they'd crossed over to the Other Side.

Curious creatures of all kinds watched soundlessly from their hiding places and though most of them harbored only good will, the men found it unnerving to feel the presence of each one. As usual, their clothes and boots were dry when they climbed onto the shore and the peculiar light of the place put them slightly off balance. Before they could comment on these phenomena, the creek froze over behind them, and the rabbit bounded away.

Seth's body transformed as soon as they entered the Other Side, confirming their suspicions if not fully explaining his origins. His tail became visible, long and thick, coiled around his body like a silver fur shield, and his lashes extended to curl over brilliant round violet eyes.

Bash said, "You could have told me."

"I could have."

Bash didn't know how they met, but ever the recruiter, Sam would have known that someone who could so easily ride the hedge between worlds would make a fantastic addition to their special unit within the sheriff's department. Of course, that person would also make an excellent a target for villainous elements on both Sides, so Bash understood Seth's reluctance to share.

Even Seth jumped though as Adira chose that moment to emerge from the shadows. The massive mountain lion greeted them with a low growl and a quick bow of the head. Time and space operated differently on the Other Side, so they weren't surprised to see her up north, and they were quite relieved that their always reluctant ally had joined them there.

Bash poked Seth with his elbow and whispered, "Another cougar."

She flicked her ears with annoyance and in their minds, they heard her voice say, "He would be wise to keep his distance from me."

They plodded two by two along the creek bank with Seth and Adira leading the way until they came upon a clearing in the trees. Adam tapped Bash on the shoulder as they passed their horses grazing in a patch of soft grass exposed by the melting snow.

"This way." Seth guided them back under cover of the trees while Adira kept her head on a swivel, looking for threats.

"One o'clock, Adam." Bash gestured to a group of three goblins perched in the trees ahead and drew his pistol. The Other Side was a violent place, but the iron in the gun was an insult to his hosts. Still, goblins held universal disdain, so no one was likely to press the issue if a few of them were weeded out with bullets. Heaven's Watch had long since proven their loyalty to the citizens of the Other Side and also, they knew that Bash did not give a shit about their precepts when his friends were in danger.

"You are an enemy of the goblins," Adira explained to Adam. "They have even put a generous bounty on your head."

"What?" Bash feigned hurt feelings. "I've killed plenty of goblins."

"They'll have to get in line for me." Adam lowered his fangs, wondering what would be worth the head of a vampire in a place that had no use for currency of any kind.

"That sure looks like a line," Seth cracked, dropping to all fours and baring his own set of sharp teeth.

Perhaps it was that there were only three of them, or the fact that it was in the interests of both Sides for them to get across quickly, but for a while it seemed as though the goblins would be satisfied with hurling pinecones and taunts as they passed.

It turned out that one of the creatures couldn't help himself and swung down to block Adam's path. The goblin managed to swipe a claw across his cheek, but Adam was even faster on the Other Side and snatched the goblin out of midair by the throat.

While it squealed and twisted in his grip, Seth said, "What happens if you drink goblin blood?"

Adam knew from the past that their blood tasted like dirty water, but it wasn't harmful and since they were on goblin turf, he wanted to make a point. He drained it swiftly and then tossed the sinewy shell at the feet of the others.

Adira shook her head in disgust as the remaining two goblins ran off screaming threats and insults. "This way. Quickly." She led them toward a tall rock wall covered in glowing petroglyphs.

Seth ran his hands along the rough surface until they sank into a soft spot large enough for him to walk through. They followed him into a damp pitch-dark cavern that echoed even the sound of their breath. They switched on their headlamps and turned in circles to get their bearings.

"I know this place," Adam said. Rotting wooden beams were lined up overhead and railcar tracks meandered throughout the tunnels.

"I thought you might," Seth said with a grin before starting back through the gateway.

"You're leaving us?" Bash said, noting that Adira had already disappeared.

"Got more logisting to do, but I'll catch you on the way back." He flashed them the peace sign and added, "Both of you, okay?"

The glistening dust particles that hovered around them fell away in a dirt cloud when Seth returned through the portal. Carl emitted something of a nervous whine, but Adam gave him a vigorous, if not reassuring, pat on the back.

"Welcome to the Copper Queen mine," he said, waving his hand in front of his face with a cough.

"What?" Bash adjusted his headlamp for a better look through the murk. "The Copper Queen has been closed for years. Laura insists on taking that weird little tour of what's left every time we come to town."

"It was closed off," Adam corrected, "not closed down."

Bash gaped over the side at what he then realized was once probably part of a huge shaft. Some narrow runged ladders half-hazzardly bolted to the walls led down the steep slope but he could not see all the way to the bottom.

"How deep in this mountain are we?"

"We're closer to the surface right now than you might think." He ran his hands along the wall until he came across a man-made hatch in the rock. "Seth dropped us in an ideal spot, but even so you'll start to feel the mine in your lungs pretty soon." He used his vampire strength to turn the spindle and pried open the heavy metal door enough to let in a slight breeze.

Confused by the traffic noise that also came through, Bash peered out of the hatch to a tin roof overhanging four cement steps that led right down to Highway 80. "I'll be damned."

"As long as you're not claustrophobic," Adam said.

"How do you know Walter will come back here?"

"Walter doesn't have a lot of ideas, Bash, and when he gets one, he can't move on. He thought I had taken over Chuparosa and made it my own personal little blood bank. He wanted to steal that utopia from me, but it never occurred to him that I would simply like living there amongst my friends."

Bash took off his hat and when he did, the attached headlamp lit up the rotting timbers above them. He put his hat back on and decided not to worry about them.

"You're thinking if he can't have Chuparosa, he'll come for Bisbee instead?"

Adam nodded. "This town is tucked away in the mountains and kind of strange already. Ideal for his purposes when you think about it."

"But Chuparosa only has fifteen hundred people. There's five thousand here in Bisbee."

"For now."

"Jesus."

"His problem is that he has no work ethic and he's never thought anything all the way through, so we've got that going for us."

"And he thinks we're hours behind him."

Adam looked at his watch. "It's gonna be light soon. I know you're tired, but I need you to do something for me."

Chapter Thirty-Four

Bash wheezed his way up Brewery Gulch to the Apex Inn wondering why every time he came to Bisbee, he was surprised that getting anywhere required a climb. Since the owners of the inn didn't live on the property, the sleeping guests were protected by a coded entry system that Adam either didn't know about or neglected to mention.

"Shit."

"Pound twenty-four, pound twenty-five, pound twenty-six."

Bash spun around to face a man loaded down by a stack of books coming out of the alley behind the Séance Room.

"You give everyone that code?" Bash asked him.

"Everyone but the guests know that code. In case there's a fire."

The man gave him a two-finger salute and sat down cross-legged to read under a light pole with a sign nailed to it that read, 'Keep Bisbee Weird'.

Bash entered the code and pushed open the creaky

door thinking that someone would get shot for that sort of thing in Chuparosa, but then again Chuparosa didn't encourage outsiders with things like hotels.

He encountered a padlock on room thirteen, but for that, Adam had given him a key. He tossed his backpack on the bed, upsetting several layers of dust on the blanket, and for a moment doubted the success of his mission.

Bisbee building codes did not allow for many upgrades to historical places, which was reflected in the reviews for the Apex Inn, but allowed Adam to assure Bash that his supplies would be exactly where he said they were. He'd also warned that the room was haunted by a prostitute, a miner and his cat who had died in their sleep during a gas leak. According to Adam, the ghosts usually minded their own business, but Bash felt the need to announce himself, nevertheless.

"I won't be long," he promised.

He gave the room an uneasy once-over and then put a small flashlight between his teeth and pulled the bed away from the wall. There, just like Adam said, was a cutout covered with a metal grate and behind the grate was a wooden case. He dragged it to the floor and transferred the entire top layer of its contents to his backpack.

Underneath the equipment were some handmade linens that divided up layers of paperwork and old sepia toned photographs. Bash left the papers and sat on the bed to flip though the pictures, letting his detective side absolve him of any pangs of guilt that arose as he pilfered through his friend's private memories.

Adam and Betty were posed amidst someone's flower garden in the first photo and Bash curled his lip at Adam's ear to ear grin. He looked so happy with her on his arm, and she was a reasonably pretty thing with blonde curls in a calico dress–he definitely had a type–but how could he not have seen the vicious glint in her eyes? A knot formed in Bash's stomach as he thought, *there but for the grace of God...*

It was difficult not to laugh out loud at the next picture of Adam and another man seated in high backed chairs in front of a tapestry background. The photographer must have told them to hold up their guns and look dangerous. The two were trying their best but they could not keep the smiles out of their eyes. Bash suspected that they might have just had a little *or a lot* to drink as well.

Both men had clearly cleaned up for the sitting, to the point where it looked almost awkward for them. They had shoulder length hair and freshly trimmed beards, but the knuckles on their calloused hands were bloodied, and on further inspection, he noticed that Adam was hiding a busted lip under his mustache. While looking for clues to the rest of the story he noticed the unnatural angle of the other man's right arm and that he held his pistol in his left hand.

"Nice to finally meet you, Jess."

He stared at the photo, studying their clothes and mannerisms, and wishing that he could have been there with them until something bounced on the bed next to him. He jumped up and though there was nothing on the bed, the clear sound of a meow echoed through the room. He carefully slid the picture of Adam and Jess into the hidden front pocket of his backpack, gave

Betty's image a sharp flick and returned the trunk to its hiding place.

Adam sat sleeping with his back to the wall, ankles crossed with Carl's upper half draped over his knees. He never stirred when Bash slipped through the narrow opening in the hatch, but his eyes flew open when Bash dropped the backpack at his feet.

"You'll want to be careful with that," Adam cautioned.

"Here." From a crumpled paper bag he handed Adam a sausage and egg sandwich and then put another one down for Carl. He emptied a water bottle into a makeshift Styrofoam bowl for the dog and gave Adam a cold canned coffee drink.

He plopped down next to them and tore into his own sandwich, wishing he'd figured out a way to carry some strong hot coffee back as he chased it with the sweet milky liquid from the convenience store cooler.

"Get some rest," Adam said, unloading the gear from the inn. "I'll wake you when it's time."

Time for what, Bash didn't want to think about, so he laid his head back against the wall and only realized he'd been sleeping all day when Carl licked his face to wake him.

"He's here." Adam stood rigid by the door to the highway.

Bash pushed himself up from his knees, moving a lot slower than he would have liked. "Sunset. He made good time."

"We're ready."

"We are?"

"Follow me." The air thickened as Adam led him down a long corridor, away from the cavern and the hatch.

"You told me once never to mess with old dynamite." Bash said.

"You're not going to." The supplies he'd gathered had been wrapped into narrow cylinders of dynamite connected by their fuses and knotted several inches apart along a section of climbing rope.

"There's not enough powder in these to even break out the rock, but I'm not using it for that." Adam explained.

Next to Adam's giant strand of makeshift firecrackers lay six perfectly carved wooden stakes. Bash gathered them into in his pack, leaving the zipper open so they were easily accessible. "What's your plan then?"

"See that chute?" At the end of the tracks was a wide metal funnel once used for transporting ore from rail cars.

Bash looked inside. "It's a long way down," he said, thinking of the rotting timbers. Even a small explosion could collapse everything and bury them alive.

"But you're going up." The bottom rungs of a ladder hung several feet above the chute. It would be quite a jump, but Adam figured Bash could probably make it, especially at a run.

"There's another ladder above that one that leads out."

"Out?"

"It's literally a hole in the mountainside covered with nothing much more than pallet slats."

Bash pondered for a moment and then got angry. "You are not blowing yourself up."

Adam ignored his concern and coiled the rope across his body. "If you hear, 'fire in the hole', you get your ass on top of that chute."

"God dammit."

"It's worst-case scenario, Sebastian. Worst case."

"Well, what about best case?"

Adam was never able to answer the question, which was just as well because he'd never believed there would be a best-case scenario—not for himself anyway. Some quiet swearing filtered into the corridor followed by the sound of the hatch door closing with an ominous thud.

"They know we're here." Bash slipped one of the stakes from his pack and they stalked out with Carl between them to meet their enemies.

As expected, Walter's men rushed them as they rounded the corner. In one of the luckiest moments of Bash's life, the vampire who tackled him began to twitch and gurgle after landing directly on the stake. Bash shrimped out from underneath him, flipped him over and pounded another stake directly into his heart. Blood spurted like a geyser from the wound, soaking both him and Carl, but he was never so grateful for such a gory mess.

Walter stood back to watch and spit some tobacco before turning his attention to Adam sparring with his minion.

"Coward," Adam gasped, putting the vampire in a chokehold, "why don't you face me?"

Walter spit again and wiped the corner of his mouth with the back of his hand.

"You think I care about them?" He gestured to his guard who was losing oxygen as they spoke.

"I hate them, and I like it when they die." He

nodded to the blood covered Bash struggling to shove the dead body into the shaft and whistled for the other vampire to go after him.

"You and me, we're different than them. This is our game-our game of life."

"This game is over," Adam snarled, "forever."

"Let's do it your way then." Having not given any thought to their aging close quarters, he plucked a large stick of dynamite from his shirt pocket and lit it up.

Adam couldn't believe Walter's stupidity. He yelled, "Fire in the hole!"

Bash heard the warning and leapt for the chute, but the vampire grabbed his legs, slamming his chest down hard on the metal. He assumed the vampire would kill him while he tried to catch his breath, but he caught another break when they were both violently jostled to opposite sides of the chute.

Walter had tossed the dynamite to Adam who batted it down the shaft. It exploded midway, collapsing the timbers around them and shaking everything loose, including the chute which crumbled along with any hope of their escape.

Adam advanced on Walter, shoving him so hard against the wall that his body left an indentation in the rock. But then he let out a howl and fell to his knees as Walter grabbed his wrist and bent back his arm, snapping it at the elbow. He took Adam's rope and unfurled it to examine the oversized firecrackers.

"Clever."

Adam rose up and lunged, knocking Walter down very near the edge of the shaft.

"Have you ever seen a man hang?" Walter asked. He jumped up and tossed the rope over what remained of the arch above the shaft, but the cracked rock gave way beneath him, and he had to grab on to the rope, clamping it between his feet to hold himself up.

Adam wasted no time, leaning out as far as he dared to light the bottom fuse. Walter's eyes widened with fear and he swung for the ledge but in seconds, the first stick of dynamite exploded and blew off his lower leg.

Screaming and cursing, he tried to climb using only the strength of his arms, but the second stick exploded before he could secure his grip. The wood beam began to crack, and he lost his hold on the loop which fell forward and slipped around his neck. His face turned red, then purple, then blue, and while he fought to free himself the next fuse ignited and blasted through his chest.

"Twice now, I've seen a man hang," Adam said, ducking away from the flying appendages.

As he ran to find Bash, Walter's last assistant jumped in front of him. He dropped into a defensive crouch, readying himself for a fight, but nearly crazed with concern for his friend. Just then, the vampire's eyes bugged out and blood spewed from his lips as a stake burst through his chest where Bash shoved it through from behind.

Bash bent over and grabbed his knees, complaining, "That's a lot harder than it looks."

Adam had been timing the crackling of the fuses between the explosions and hollered, "Get down!" just as the blast shook them off their feet. A blunt force hit Adam's torso and what he thought was a chunk of stone turned out to be Walter's severed head bouncing off his back. The head rolled around; its expression locked in mid-scream until Adam kicked it down the shaft.

They could not take shelter in the collapsing corridor and the hatch was blocked by debris, so they ran to where the chute once was.

Bash looked up in dismay. "There's no way I can reach the ladder now."

Adam crouched and intertwined his fingers for Bash to step up. Though his wrist was broken, he gritted his teeth and tossed Bash with as much aim as he could manage. Bash grabbed the lowest rung of the ladder with one hand, growling a string of unintelligible curses as he pulled himself up.

Adam scooped Carl in his broken arm and jumped, catching a rung close on Bash's heels. Little aftershocks rattled the wall and the rusted bolts holding the ladder began to come away from the rock.

"Go!" Adam guided the dog in front of Bash when he made it to the second ladder and then had to jump again to reach it himself as the first ladder came loose and fell.

At the top Carl scuttled through the space between the wooden slats, barking furiously when he got out as if it would make the men climb faster. Bash wouldn't fit between the slats and had to make a bigger hole by ramming the wood with his shoulder. He reached back and hauled Adam out with all that was left of his strength and were it not for a cluster of sticker bushes, they both would have slid down the side of the mountain.

Instead, they rolled on their backs, quietly assessing their damage while Carl paced between them.

After some time, Adam asked, "Are you okay?"

Bash propped himself up on his elbow and grumbled, "Next time we plan for the best-case scenario."

His broken arm began to itch and as it healed, a bit of levity came over Adam and he started to laugh.

"What's so funny?"

A small chunk of green-tinged copper ore poked out of Bash's collar. Adam couldn't tell if they'd blown it from the rock or if they'd somehow picked up an old piece on the way up. "You're a miner now." He handed it over. "Give this to Laura."

Chapter Thirty-Five

Sam had gone to work on Rance in the Medevac helicopter before they'd even reached the hospital. It didn't take much to convince the young man that driving a truck would never hold the same appeal unless he paired that skill with a career in supernatural law enforcement; and after being fed on and tortured himself, Rance felt a certain responsibility to those who were not equipped to fight back.

At the hunter's shack, he and Sam stood by while Doug plowed a deep grave with the mini excavator. As they severed the heads from the dead vampires, *just in case*, and dumped them in, Seth appeared from behind a nearby boulder.

"Did you have any trouble getting them back home? Sam asked.

"Nah," Seth shook his head. "We went through the portal behind the honey store, and it was mostly smooth sailing."

"Mostly?"

"Let's just say that those harpies are less uppity now

and Adam won't need a drink anytime soon."

"Literally two birds with one stone." Sam laughed.

"Bash was not amused." Seth gave Sam a rueful look, "I'd stay out of his way for a while."

"I believe Seth might have known all along that those harpies were gonna cause trouble."

"Might have known?" Bash dusted himself off and repositioned his hat. "That fucker."

They'd fallen out of a portal in one of the Palo Verde trees that lined the south side of Adam's yard and Bash smiled wide as he eyed Laura's Jeep in the driveway.

Resisting the urge to run to her, he stood with his friend while Adam hesitated at the edge of the property. Earlier, Adam had spoken about feeling an unexpected sense of freedom with Walter gone, a lightness of being that he'd not known in over a century. That joy was tempered by his fear of losing Cara. He wanted so much for them to start a new chapter together, but what did she want?

"Do you think—"

"You have to go inside if you want answers," Bash prodded gently.

Just then Laura bolted out the door and threw her arms around him. "You're about to find out." Bash gestured to Cara who stood at the threshold, thin and small.

Even after two blood transfusions, she hadn't completely healed. Her blonde hair hung limp and dull at her shoulders and the skin around her eyes was so dark that her soft gray irises seemed to glow an eerie white. She lowered them when he looked her way and held the doorjamb to steady herself as he went to her. He moved so slowly that she thought maybe he wasn't really there at all until finally he stepped on to the porch.

"Adam..." She didn't dare reach for him, though his closeness overwhelmed her senses. "There's nothing I can say to make it right. I should never have..." Her voice cracked and her shoulders sagged. "I wish that somehow we could just start over."

She wouldn't meet his eyes, so he lifted her chin. "I thought I could forget about the past and just live here in the now with you. But we are our memories, Cara, especially devils like us. I should have told you everything."

A cry escaped her throat as he pulled her into his arms, asking, "Do you love me?"

Her body shook with sobs, so she could only sniffle and nod, but that was all he needed. He relaxed his arms around her, kissed her forehead and stroked her hair.

"Then we start over right now."

* * *

"I've been thinking about something," Laura said. Wearing only her bra and panties, she stood in the closet deciding between two dresses as they got ready to have dinner at Adam and Cara's house.

"Me too." Bash lounged on their bed and pumped his eyebrows at her.

"I'm serious." She tossed him a shirt, pulled a dark blue cotton dress over her head, and made her way to the dresser where Bash had laid the picture of Adam and Jess.

He stood and buttoned up the soft brown flannel she'd selected for him. "I know, I'm gonna give that back to him tonight."

She studied the photo for a few seconds and asked, "Have you ever looked into your ancestry?"

"Hell, I don't like most of the family I *do* know." He thought for a moment before reconsidering. "That's not entirely true. Except for Nick, the Scott's are for shit, but sometimes I wish I knew more about my mother's side. Why?"

He followed her to the closet in the guest bedroom and helped her pull down a box labeled KEEP.

"Those are my mom's things," he said. "I don't really know what all is in there, but I don't want to get rid of it."

Bash missed his mother terribly and had avoided going through the box since her death. Laura carefully removed the lid and poked through the items until she found what she'd been certain she would: a small square metal cookie tin that contained a stack of pictures.

They were mostly of Bash, and she laughed, holding up one of him as a lanky teenager, and then one of his mother, rocking him as a baby in their shabby but meticulously clean apartment.

"Warren must have taken this." Bash's voice hardened on his father's name, but his eyes reddened at the sight of his mother, so Laura quickened her pace.

What she wanted was near the bottom of the stack, under faded, pink-edged polaroids of young Lilly Scott. Lilly was lovely, wearing what would be Bash's ear to ear grin in almost every frame. Then in a small protective sheet of brown paper she found two sepia toned images of a tall man with a dark-haired woman at his side. Even through the beard, that smile was unmistakable.

Bash sucked in his breath as Laura laid the picture on the bed next to Adam's. Jess was in both photos and there was no doubt about it.

Scrawled on the back of his mother's photo were the words, 'Me and Cory-January 1897'.

"Jess wrote this." Bash ran his thumb reverently over the inscription.

Laura unfolded Lilly's death certificate. "Her maiden name was Carson, Bash." She wondered how he had missed that detail.

Bash sat down hard on the bed. In truth he'd wondered about it with a tiny spark of hope when Adam first mentioned that he reminded him of Jess. Laura was right and after everything they'd been through, his reluctance to mix fantasy with reality was laughable, but he'd still not allowed himself to believe it was possible.

"My god." Adam turned the pictures over and over in his hands. "Can you believe this, darlin'?"

Cara blushed. Adam had never settled on a pet name for her before, and Laura smiled thinking that the simplicity of darlin' suited their humble rebeginning.

It was going to be a long recovery on all fronts. Physically healed at last, Cara had developed a touch of agoraphobia since her kidnapping and Laura noticed that even while opening a bottle of wine, she never allowed herself to be more than arms reach away from Adam. Still, the spark was returning to her eyes, and she'd agreed tentatively to run errands in Phoenix with Laura the following week.

"She was so beautiful," Cara gushed, holding up the picture. Cory's long braided hair hung over her shoulder, just above her waist. "And look at that dress—what color do you think it was?"

"Cory was a pistol," Adam chuckled, "but damn he loved her."

Bash stole a glance at Laura, muttering to himself, "Some things never change."

"Jess was my brother in every way but blood and some of my best memories were in this crazy town with him and Cory," Adam said, "and that's why I came back." He kissed the top of Cara's hand. "I knew if I was going to be happy, it would be here, but," his gaze traveled once again from the pictures to Bash, "I had no idea I would find the rest of my family too."

"This is Chuparosa, Adam." Cara said, linking arms with Laura. "It's a hard place. But you should know by now that Chuparosa *always* takes care of its own."

Epilogue

"How sweet." Lucifer thought. From his perch on a fence post outside of Adam's house, he and the three-foot rabbit watched through the window as the couples enjoyed their dinner. He could have told them that Jess Carson was Sebastian's great, great grandfather, but it had been more fun to watch them work it out for themselves.

Contrary to popular belief, he really did prefer happy endings, and this one was particularly so. The uncanny little group had succeeded once again. They had all earned his respect, but he particularly liked Laura. Her intensity would be an asset, but she was appropriately suspicious, and he would have to use more caution with her in the future.

They had succeeded with no thanks to Thomas. Wherever he was, Laura and Company no doubt felt abandoned by him, and that would make it easier for Lucifer to move forward with his plans.

As if able to read his thoughts, the rabbit bared its teeth at him and though he fluffed his wings and showed his own menacing snarl, it stood its ground. The Other Side would surely make things more complicated, but their uses outweighed their troublesome antics.

One by one, he finally had a chance to rid Hell of its most annoying prisoners and then focus on the only thing that had ever mattered to him: getting home. He had a plan for that too, but everything would depend on winning their trust.

Though known as the father of lies, he only ever told the truth. Truth that most humans simply could not bear to hear. His honesty would be essential for their upcoming mission and while they might not like it, he was certain that Heaven's Watch could handle it.

About the Author

Vanessa Haney grew up in rural Arizona with, tragically, no access to the Other Side. Had there been a portal, she would have gone through it a long time ago. Instead, she makes a happy life in less rural Arizona with her son Connor, her partner Mike and a black cat named Felix. There she writes, hikes and watches way too many horror movies.

Sign up to follow her adventures at:
http://www.vanessahaneywrites.com